WESTERN SEDUCTION

BRENDA JERNIGAN

AWARD WINNING AUTHOR

SCOTT PUBLISHING

COPYRIGHT

DEDICATION

"Special thanks to Bonnie Gardner, Julie Lence, Rebecca York, and Pat Rice.
This book is dedicated to all the fans who have waited for book 2 of the Seduction Series. Hope you enjoy."

EXCERPT

Shannon McKinley flees Scotland to America hoping for a new life. She has answered an ad to be a nanny at Star Ranch in the Texas Territory. It doesn't matter that she has never been a nanny. If she can handle men...she can handle children. As Shannon tames Luke Griffin's two wild children, Luke proves a little more difficult as he still mourns his dead wife. Shannon will never accept being second best. As she begins to melt the ice from Luke's heart, can he really let the past go and take a chance on love?

When a feisty Scot steps out of the stage in Cottonwood, Texas, Luke Griffin can do nothing but stare. He advertised for old and ugly, but this woman doesn't fit that description at all. And she is much too small to survive in Texas. He will send her back on the next stage. But for now, Luke will take her to the ranch and ignore the heat that runs though his veins every time she is near him.

In this wild and rugged land, will Shannon's dark secret endanger the family she has come to love?

PRAISE FOR BRENDA JERNIGAN

Brenda's books have been a finalist
Booksellers Best Award
Holt Medallion Award
Maggie Award

"Ms. Jernigan writes adventure and magic."
Publishers Weekly

"Ms. Jernigan takes an old plot and makes it fresh and exciting." Rendezvous Magazine

"Ms. Jernigan writes her stories with a true flair for love and romance." A Romance Review

"Tender love story with a feisty heroine, a rugged hero and charming children. Don't miss it!" Joan Johnston - NY Times Bestselling Author

"A passionate, witty, delightful read...filled with snappy dialogue and great characters. I couldn't put it down. A definite keeper." Fiona Hood-Steward

"As usual her characters are interesting, her plot action-packed, and her love story filled with conflict and emotion. A great read from a talented writer." Rendezvous Magazine

"Cassie Edwards' readers are sure to find Brenda Jernigan irresistible ..." Rhapsody Debut Author - Rhapsody Book Club

"Brenda Jernigan has written an emotionally touching novel that tugs the heartstrings in all the right ways. I fell in love with all the characters. This is truly a fantastic read that should be savored and enjoyed over and over again. I look forward to many more books from this wonderful author." Interludes Magazine

"Don't start this one until you are sure you will have plenty of time to read. You won't want to put it down. AWESOME! Highly recommended!" Huntress Reviews

PRAISE FOR WESTERN SEDUCTION

Nominated for a RONE Award – Best Western

"Brenda Jernigan has given the reader two characters that are fiery, strong, and sure to bring fireworks both out of the sheets and between them." Lynn-Alexandria McKendrick - InD'tale Magazine

"Author Brenda Jernigan paints a vivid portrait of the early West that almost made me feel as if I were there. Romance, Adventure, and some historical bits thrown into the mix make this story just too good to miss. I cannot recommend this tale highly enough." Detra Fitch Huntress Reviews

"This is a book for you to read if you like western romance. It's well-written and a fast read that you don't want to put down!" Marilyn McDonald-Mahuron

"A fiery Scot and a hunky rancher add up for some fun in Brenda Jernigan's latest release, Western Seduction. Toss in two villains, a stampede and the children's antics, then step back in time and enjoy a story sure to have you laughing and cheering and falling in love." Julie Lence

"Fabulous book! A feisty Scot always makes for a fun read, then add a hot, hot, hot sexy cowboy and whoa mama! (Can you tell I like? Lol) Shannon has a lot to prove to Luke if she's gonna stay on his ranch and take care of his two young children. This really is a wonderfully fun book to read. Lots of action and adventure to keep you involved. I'm reading book #1 in this series next, and can't wait for book #3, by Brenda Jernigan." Amazon Reviewer

"This book has everything I love in a storyline. Shannon is the nanny from Scotland that Luke hired but....not exactly. She is not old, ugly and easily forgotten. What arrived on the stage was a fiery, young beauty, with a temper to match. The story itself is engaging and full of adventure. You add a couple darling children to the mix and it's a winner. I also love the fact that the book can stand alone or be enjoyed as part of a series. " Nicole Laverdure Reviewer

PROLOGUE

allander Castle, Scotland

ANGUS McKINLEY WAS NOT a patient man.

He sat in the Great Hall and stared at his tankard, trying hard to control the rage that built in him like a simmering cauldron waiting to boil.

The lass had defied him. By God, he would teach her a lesson once he had his hands on her again.

Shannon had slipped away in the middle of the night and he had been none the wiser until late the next day. Angus gulped a swallow of mead then slammed the tankard back on the table, ignoring the mead that sloshed over the sides.

When he found Shannon he would beat her to within an inch of her life. But he'd be careful not to scar that lovely face of hers as he needed her beauty for her marriage. The marriage he had arranged with Buchanan.

Drumming his fingers on the brown trestle table, Angus

wondered what he was going to say to Buchanan. Angus had promised Shannon to the laird in exchange for cattle and wealth to help his struggling clan.

He thought he had the girl under control. The night before he'd blacked her eye for talking back to him, and then he locked her in her room. Damn, Douglas. Angus thought he could trust the clansman, but the bastard had helped his daughter escape.

When his men had caught up with Douglas they had brought him back to the castle.

Douglas had been reluctant to talk, but after he'd been put on the rack his tongue had loosened. He said he'd taken Shannon to her English uncle, The Duke of Devonshire, so Angus couldn't hurt her anymore.

Angus was so angry he'd killed Douglas on the spot.

Angus hadn't been able to get the girl with the Duke's protection, until now. Luck was on his side. News had arrived two weeks ago that the Duke of Devonshire had died.

Now was his chance.

Angus turned as two men strode across the Great Hall, the rushes snapping under their boots. They cleared their throats as they neared the end of the very long table, interrupting Angus's reverie.

"Where is the lass?" Angus demanded.

"She has boarded a ship tae America," Alasdair said.

"When we got there, the ship had just sailed," Callum added.

"Then by God, ye need tae be on the next ship! Shannon must be brought home. She has a duty tae her da and her clan."

1

Texas Territory 1835

'Twas never good to lie . . . but sometimes necessary, Shannon McKinley reasoned.

Even if it was only a small lie . . . Well, in *her* eyes, 'twas small. Yet the farther Shannon traveled into this unknown land, the more she doubted her own sanity.

Suddenly, the stagecoach hit a rut, sending her and the other two passengers up to the roof and back down with resounding thuds. Shannon's bottom was now numb after two days of riding in this wooden crate.

She'd never dreamed the Texas Territory was so far away from civilization. She'd been gazing out the window most of the day and hadn't seen anything that remotely resembled human life. Then again, perhaps, isolation was better for her because Mr. Griffin couldn't easily put her on a train if he was displeased that his mail-order nanny was much younger than what he'd advertised for.

Had it really been three weeks since she'd bid her cousin Jocelyn goodbye in New York? If Shannon closed her eyes, she could still picture Jocelyn and Brooke as the three of them stood by the rail of the ship, wondering what America would hold for them. Each of them had wanted their own adventure in America after leaving England. However, Shannon hadn't realized her adventure would take forever to begin.

The stagecoach hit another hole in the dirt road, but she didn't complain. What good would it do? However, she couldn't say the same about her two matronly traveling companions. They had complained constantly and were now threatening to lynch Shorty, their driver.

"I do believe Shorty has hit every blessed rock and hole in the road since we left Louisiana," Thelma complained as she straightened her sky-blue bonnet which kept slipping farther sideways with every bounce. "Why we have to ride in a mail coach is beyond me."

Emma glanced at her sister. "Possibly 'cause it's the only transportation into the Texas Territory other than on horseback and you, sister dear, have trouble walking, much less riding. You wouldn't last a mile on a horse."

"I'll have you know that I'm still younger than you, Emma dear," Thelma protested. "So don't you go getting uppity on me. I'd probably do just fine."

"You're only younger by two years. You'll be seventy before you know it. Remember, with age comes wisdom."

Shannon listened to the two elderly sisters bicker. She was growing accustomed to their bickering. It seemed to be what they liked to do best, and their presence most certainly had made the long trip much more bearable.

Thelma and Emma Miller were spinsters who lived with a third sister in Cottonwood. Together they ran the dry goods store. If these women were sixty-eight and seventy, Shannon wondered how old their other sister, Rose, was. However, if all the town's residents were as boisterous as these two, life would be very interesting in Cottonwood.

Shannon tried to make herself comfortable on the hard bench seat. If it hadn't been for the good sisters, she would've ended up wandering lost around St. Louis after she'd gotten off the train. She was looking for a coach similar to the ones they had back home -- something sleek and black with soft cushions instead of this hard wood. However, she'd quickly discovered the only way to get to the Texas Territory was by mail coach or horseback.

She glanced out the window. "Ye know, I've not seen any sign o' life all day. Are ye sure somebody lives out here?"

Thelma chuckled. "This is the West, honey. The Texas Territory is just being settled, and we're probably lucky we ain't run into any Indians by now. You know, it's still a part of Mexico, not the United States. Still, the Americans outnumber the Mexican settlers now, and there's talk of independence."

"I huv tae admit I dinna know much about yer country. 'Tis my first time in America."

"You'll learn, dear," Thelma said, patting her knee.

Emma reached over and touched Shannon's hand. "Well, we're mighty glad to have you," Emma said. "Don't hear many odd accents around here. Where did you say you're from, dear?"

Shannon smiled at Emma before answering. "Scotland," she said proudly, appreciating the woman's motherly ways.

"Do you have family in Cottonwood?" Emma asked.

"No. I've accepted a job tae be the nanny fer Mr. Griffin's children."

"The Griffin children," both women said at the same time.

Shannon nodded.

Thelma and Emma exchanged wide-eyed looks. "You poor thing," Thelma said.

"Why do ye say that?"

Thelma shook her head. "Those youngsters are a handful."

"Their ma died two years ago, poor things," Emma added. "And since then they have been through six nannies."

"Interesting," Shannon said. She'd been a little concerned when the women had given each other funny looks, but what children were not a handful? "I'm sure 'tis hard on them without their mother."

"It is," Thelma agreed with a nod. "Their father could be the problem, though. You see, Luke loved his wife very much. Never seen a man so dedicated. He still mourns Ruth."

"'Tis perfectly common tae mourn a loved one."

"Don't know of any man mourning for two years." Thelma arched her fine brow. "Especially with young'uns."

Emma shifted and glanced quickly around as if someone were eavesdropping on them. "Now, I'm not one to gossip, you understand." She paused and waited for Shannon to nod before proceeding. "I think Luke pushes his children away from him because they remind him of their mother."

"'Tis verra sad," Shannon murmured with a sorrowful shake of her head. What would it be like to have a man love her like Mr. Griffin loved his wife? She sighed, figuring she'd never know.

Her da had told her more than once that no man would

want someone who was as homely as she was. Especially with her god-awful red hair. Shannon pushed his words away and concentrated on the present. "What happened tae their mother?"

"Ruth came from back East and was used to city life. She was too delicate to live in Texas and couldn't adjust to the harsh environment. Must say, she stayed sick all the time. And then one day, Ruth took to her bed and never got up again," Emma said with a sad shake of her head. "She was such a pretty little thing."

"Surprises me that Luke would hire you," Thelma interjected. "You're mighty small yourself."

"But I'm not frail," Shannon informed them.

They both raised their eyebrows in doubt.

"'Tis true. I'm a bit tougher than I appear." Shannon insisted with a defiant tilt of her chin.

Emma reached over and patted Shannon's knee again. "We sure hope so. However, if things get bad for you, you're welcome to come and stay with us for a spell. We like you."

Shannon smiled her thanks to the kind ladies, then turned to stare out the window. Just how bad could it get? she wondered. Were the children truly holy terrors?

Mr. Griffin's letter had said his children were adorable. Could he have lied just as she had lied to him?

"We'll be in Cottonwood in about an hour, ladies," Shorty shouted from up top. She was sure Shorty must have a last name, but since arriving in St. Louis, she heard many men referred to by some nickname or other. Nothing formal like she was used to, and she definitely hadn't heard any titles. It seemed no one here had one.

She remembered one man at the St. Louis post office was referred to as Rattlesnake. Shannon didn't want to know how he'd earned such a name. Just the sound of it made her shiver. She hated snakes.

She most certainly was going to make sure she didn't end up with a nickname. Several strangers had already called her Red because of her hair, which she hadn't appreciated at all.

She could be touchy about her hair. God must have given her this odd color for some reason, but she'd yet to figure out why.

Just another hour, Shannon thought with relief, then she could get out of these cramped quarters. She turned back to the window and gazed at the countryside. The land wasn't exactly what she'd pictured. It was nothing like the beautiful, lush green hills in her Highlands. Instead, what she'd seen of Texas was brown and flat with few trees. And the dust . . . that was definitely something she would have to get used to. Even now, the temperatures were much warmer than she was accustomed to, and it was autumn. She wondered what summers were like in Texas if it was still hot.

Mr. Griffin had come to live in Texas from St. Louis, so he must have seen something promising in this land. What would Mr. Griffin be like? Pleasant, she hoped. From his letters and what the sisters had said, he sounded like a nice man who had cared for his wife. His penmanship had been beautiful, so she figured he was educated. However, she wasn't going to worry about Mr. Griffin for the moment. Shannon would do as she always had: face the problem head on once it presented itself. For all she knew, Emma and Thelma could be exaggerating.

Besides, if Shannon could handle men and their childish ways, she was sure she could handle one heartbroken rancher and his children. Two children shouldn't be that difficult.

Strange, she thought, she was traveling through hostile land, yet she felt safe. Way out here, her father would never be able to find her. And that was the way she wanted it. Just the thought of Angus McKinley made her shudder as though she were cold. 'Twas hard to believe that he was her da. He'd never shown her any kind of love. Just the opposite. He was a cruel mon.

Her mother had been English and her father was a Highlander, so, of course, the Highlands were where she'd grown up. Shannon couldn't say that she'd had a happy childhood. Most of it had been spent in fear of her drunken, domineering da. She could remember begging her mother to leave their home, but she had insisted that it was her duty to stay.

Angus was a mean drunk, bullying the weak and the small. Elizabeth, Shannon's mother, had tried to protect her from being beaten, and most of the time she'd been successful, hiding Shannon when Angus was in a foul mood.

However, the morning she'd found her mother lying cold and still at the foot of the stone stairs, Shannon knew her father had been responsible. He claimed he'd never touched Elizabeth, and maybe he hadn't, but she was still dead. He'd pointed out that her mother might have tripped on her gown and fallen during the night, but Shannon had seen the bruises on her mother's arms and around her neck, and she knew...

Shannon had felt guilty that her mother had suffered and she hadn't been able to help her. Perhaps, if she'd been with her mother, she could have pushed Angus away, and then he'd have been the one at the foot of the stairs.

Things had grown worse after her mother's death. When

Shannon was alone with her da, she had endured the beatings her mother had protected her from. However, once she'd turned seventeen, something in her had snapped, and she'd warned her da that if he ever placed a hand on her again she would kill him.

He had simply laughed.

But she'd meant every word.

It didn't take long for Shannon to realize that Angus could easily kill *her* before she had a chance to defend herself. So she ran with the help of Douglas, one of her da's men, who'd enabled her escape to England. Later she learned that Douglas had been killed when Angus had discovered his ruse.

In England she'd found refuge with her uncle Jackson Montgomery, Duke of Devonshire. Jackson, her mother's brother, had been a good man.

"Why are you frowning so, dear?" Thelma asked.

Slowly, Shannon turned from the window. She felt dead inside when she thought of her da. "I was thinkin' about my home."

Emma shifted over to the other bench so she could sit beside Shannon. She slipped an arm around her shoulders. "It's only natural that you'll be homesick."

Shannon gave the women a small smile. There was little chance that she'd be homesick. Nonetheless, she remained mum. She didn't want to explain her past to women she barely knew.

"What the hell!" Shorty swore from up top.

Shannon glanced out the window. "Looks like a town up ahead."

The stage pulled to an abrupt stop, nearly throwing her from her seat. Dust swirled around the stage so thickly that Shannon had to jerk her head back inside to avoid a mouth full of grit.

Thelma peered out the window on her side. "I believe we're finally home," she said. "But I wonder why Shorty stopped way out here on the edge of town? The post office is down the road a ways."

They didn't have long to wonder because Shorty yanked open the door. "Ladies, appears there's a gunfight going on in town, so we better not get too close. Wouldn't want to see anybody hurt or nothing."

"A gunfight?" Thelma said, stepping out of the stage, followed by Emma, who added, "What in the world . . ."

"Ladies! Get back in the stage!" Shorty barked.

Well, Shannon surely wasn't going to stay in this stuffy box one minute longer than she had to, so she followed the ladies out the door.

Shorty grumbled and hastened alongside her.

Shannon's steps quickened. It appeared that her quest for excitement was already starting . . . a real live gunfight.

They moved down the boardwalk, careful not to get in danger's way, but close enough that they could see what was happening. Sure enough, two men were squaring off in the middle of the street and there was a crowd gathered on the boardwalks to watch.

The man whose back was to her was several inches taller than his opponent. He made a striking figure from behind. His shirt stretched across his broad shoulders and he was dressed all in black. Usually, the bad guy wore black, or so she'd read. This was certainly how she'd pictured a cowboy to look.

"I wonder why they are fightin'?" Shannon asked.

"Could be anything," Shorty answered. "Sometimes it's just the way a man looks at you."

Emma and Thelma strolled over to stand beside them. "This isn't the way we'd like to introduce you to our little town, but out here men and guns are plentiful, so I guess you'd best get used to it, honey."

"'Tis the same at home," Shannon said. "Only 'tis broad swords they use fer weapons." She glanced back at the combatants in the middle of the dusty dirt street. "After this is over, I'll huv tae send word tae Mr. Griffin that I've arrived."

Emma gave her a strange smile. "No need, honey."

Confused, Shannon turned to Emma. Something vaguely disturbing tugged at her, warning her that she wasn't going to like the answer to her next question. "Why?"

"Because Luke Griffin is the tall one out there." Emma nodded toward the street. "He's the one dressed in black."

Speechless, Shannon let her gaze wander over the man. She became aware of the tension and energy about his body that made her think of an animal ready to attack.

So this was her employer. Was the mon crazy? He could be killed and leave his children orphaned. He could be killed and she'd be without a job.

Then what would she do?

2

_____

*H*e didn't have time for this shit.

Luke Griffin strode onto the dirt road which was now considered Cottonwood's Main Street. Hell, when he'd first come to this town there had only been one building and no streets. Now Cottonwood was a booming town with ten buildings and one street. However, along with growth came men like Tom Shank, a young gunslinger looking to make a name for himself.

Unfortunately for Shank, he'd picked the wrong man this time 'cause Luke was in a real bad mood, and he wasn't backing down.

Why some men wouldn't forget about his past, Luke didn't know. He was a rancher now. He had a family. What had happened before needed to stay in the past, but some people never forgot.

Usually Luke tried to talk the fools itching for a fight out of gunplay, but this idiot had shot one of his ranch hands in the arm for no good reason. And since Luke was already in a bad mood, it didn't take much to push him into a fight.

Someone had rustled five of his steers this morning, and

if that wasn't bad enough, the nanny he'd hired for his children had yet to arrive. She should have been here a month ago. Where in the Sam Hill she was he didn't know. He didn't have the time to track her whereabouts or the patience to keep his children out of trouble and run a ranch, too.

Luke stopped once he reached the middle of the street, then turned and faced the gunslinger. He should be afraid, but he wasn't. Fear was something a man felt when he wasn't sure of his ability. That wasn't the case with Luke. The man walking toward him had come to kill for no good reason except to add a notch on his belt.

Tom Shank stopped and took position, hand hovering over the Colt strapped around his hip. He flexed his fingers as he waited, trying to intimidate his opponent.

Luke didn't intimidate.

He wondered how many men the kid had killed, but it didn't really matter. He wasn't about to let him add any more to his count. He scanned the boardwalks, remembering Shank had ridden into town with two other men. The moment Luke thought of them, he knew they were hidden somewhere, poised to make sure if Shank went down, so would his opponent – mainly, him.

Luke spotted one of the sidewinders in the shadows, rifle in hand, lifting it to take aim. He didn't wait to see what the fellow's intentions were; he fired one shot over Shank's head, and the other man hit the ground. Even from this distance, Luke saw Shank quivering.

So much for his courage.

Without pausing to think, Luke swung and fired at the second shadow. At the same moment, he heard a burst of gunfire coming from his right, so he went down on one knee and fired toward the sound, taking out a third man, one he hadn't recalled seeing before.

Shank had gotten to his feet and stood glaring at him. Luke saw him flex a split-second before Shank went for his gun. He was fast, but Luke was faster. He crouched and fired, taking the gunslinger out.

For a moment, there was no sound, nothing but silence, reminding Luke of the many times in his youth that he'd been in this same spot before, facing gunslingers looking to kill just for the fun of it.

A chill skittered down his spine. Thank goodness that kind of life was behind him. He didn't want it anymore. He'd tried to move on. If only the rest of the world would let him.

The good people of Cottonwood spilled out into the street from the safety of their stores and shops to see what had happened close up and to ask Luke if he was all right.

"I'm fine, Ralph," Luke told the undertaker, who was the first to reach him. "Look, I'll pay for their wooden boxes. Guess everybody deserves a final resting place. Theirs will be Cottonwood."

Someone placed a hand on his arm and Luke swung around, ready to fight. It was Lois, the woman who ran the only place where a man could get a decent meal in these parts.

"Are you all right, honey?" she asked, concern evident in her voice.

He knew Lois was sweet on him, and she was nice enough, he supposed. It would be an easy solution to some of his problems to marry her. Then his children would have a mother to care for them, but it wouldn't be right to do that to Lois. Luke didn't think he could ever have feelings for anyone again. He still loved Ruth, his late wife, and doubted he'd ever find another woman like her.

Realizing he hadn't answered Lois, Luke took a breath and said, "Yeah, I'm fine." He looked around. "Sorry you folks had to see this, but it's all over now."

"They were out lookin' for trouble. Wer'n't nothin' you could do to stop 'em," Ralph said.

"Doesn't mean I have to like it." Luke rubbed the back of his neck, aching to get the kinks out. All of a sudden he felt tired, damned tired. "I'd best get my supplies and head back to the ranch. I don't need any more trouble today."

Luke's foreman strode over. "That's the damnedest thing I've ever seen," Wilson said. "And the very reason I work for you, boss," he added with a smile.

Luke quirked his brow. "I thought you worked for me 'cause I pay you handsomely," he drawled dryly. "Let's head back."

"Look." Wilson pointed toward the outskirts of town. "There's the mail coach. Might as well stay and check the mail while we're here."

Luke turned and glanced toward the stage. Shorty ushered his passengers back toward the mail coach then climbed back up to the driver's seat.

"I've finished loading the wagon," Luke told Wilson then added, "If you'll bring it over to the post office, I'll meet you there. Did Doc tend to your wound?"

"Yeah, boss. Said I was lucky the bullet just tore the flesh."

"Good." Luke nodded as he watched Shorty open the stage door. "I see the Miller sisters have returned to town," he commented. "I'll get the mail. Maybe I'll have some word as to why my nanny hasn't shown up yet."

～

"Okay, ladies, back in the stage," Shorty yelled. "I'll take you on to the depot. Won't be but a minute or two."

"'Tis sae close, can we not walk the distance?" Shannon asked, having no desire to climb back into the rickety box.

"Nope. Can't do it." Shorty shook his head. "It's my dang job to take you to your proper destination along with the mail. You don't want me gettin' in trouble, do you?" he asked with eyebrows raised.

"I suppose not," Shannon said with a sigh as she climbed back into the small compartment, which she'd hoped never to see again. The stage lurched into motion.

A wave of apprehension swept through Shannon, but she didn't have long to think about it because they had reached the post office. She had wanted adventure, but somehow her stomach had forgotten that brave statement and was twisting itself into knots. Of course, she'd never expected to see anything like what she'd just witnessed. It was different from home -- people fighting for apparently no good reason.

Smoothing her fingers over her taffeta skirt, Shannon wondered how she was going to adjust to this strange land so different from home. Still, she sensed that below the surface many things were the same in Texas as in her homeland. The violence she'd witnessed in the street was a part of this life.

She'd read about gunfights. She just hadn't expected to see one so soon. It was frightening in person, especially when her employer was involved. But then, Shannon thought, she could handle just about anything as long as it kept her away from her da.

She straightened her green jacket, hoping to appear like a professional nanny who knew what she was doing. Her hair was twisted into a tight knot to make her look older, and she tried to look prim and proper by holding her head high, her chin up.

The door to the coach swung open. "Ladies, welcome to Cottonwood," Shorty said with a smile. Then he added, "Again."

Emma and Thelma climbed clumsily out of the stage, but Shannon held back for a moment so she could observe the townspeople before they noticed her. Immediately, she saw Luke Griffin, her new employer, who apparently had come to greet the stage. She didn't think he'd come to meet her since she was over a month late.

Mr. Griffin's tall, lean body was clothed in a casual style that was nothing like what proper Englishmen wore, yet his black trousers seemed very appropriate in this setting. His hair was thick and unfashionably long, but it most certainly looked grand on him. The color was different – not brown nor blond, perhaps the color of a hickory nut described it best. Shannon wished she could see his eyes. Uncle Jackson had always said one could tell the cut of a man by looking into his eyes, and apparently he had been right.

"Shorty," Luke said with a curt nod. At the sound of his voice, Shannon felt an odd sort of chill. His voice was rich, deep, and commanding. "Do you have some mail for us?"

"Yep," Shorty said, then reached for two brown mail sacks. "Got you a bigger package, too." He grinned, adding, "Just glad you're around to take it." He tossed the bags to Luke. "That fellow get you riled up?"

Luke caught the leather satchels. "Just somebody looking to make a name for himself. This time he looked in the wrong place."

Dangerous, Shannon thought. This was a man who killed and then went about his business as if it were no different than giving Shorty the time of day. So why did she find Mr. Griffin so fascinating? Could she be a bit daft?

"Well, we are mighty glad to have you around to protect the townsfolk," Emma said.

Luke swung toward them. Shannon could see there was an inherent strength in his face. "I haven't taken the job of sheriff yet, ladies. I do what I can. If it were up to me there would be no gunplay. I've seen more than enough in my life."

"At least one of your worries are over," Thelma told him.

Luke's brow shot up. "Oh?"

"We've brought the nanny for your children."

"Well, it's about damn time! Excuse me, ladies," Luke apologized. "Where is she?" he turned and looked behind him to make sure he hadn't walked past her. That made Shannon smile.

"Still in the carriage," Emma said with a swing of her hand.

Mr. Griffin frowned. "Does she need help getting out?"

"Don't be shy, Shannon, dear," Emma called. "Come on out and meet Luke."

Shannon took a deep breath, gathered her skirts and slid across the bench toward the door. She took the hand that was offered to her only to find, once she had touched the ground, it was Luke to whom the hand belonged.

In that brief instant as their eyes met, Shannon realized Luke was a commanding figure, indeed. Not only did she see determination in his gaze, but also sadness that he probably hid most of the time.

Suddenly, she felt hot all over as if someone had lit a match to her toes, and it had nothing to do with the weather in Texas. Mr. Griffin stared at her openly, and his frank assessment made her squirm. In spite of her uneasiness, Shannon noticed that his eyes were green like hers. Something told her he also had a temper to match her own.

This could be a problem.

Shannon removed her hand from his and took a step back to put a little distance between them. "Mr. Griffin, I'm Shannon McKinley, your new nanny."

Mr. Griffin didn't say a word. Instead, he gazed at her for several long, silent moments, searching every inch of her face. For what he was looking, she didn't know. Still, she didn't flinch. "Don't ye know 'tis impolite tae stare?"

He still didn't answer.

"Do ye not huv a tongue, mon?"

"I agree with the child," Thelma scolded. "You are being rude, Luke Griffin! I'm sure Shannon must be hungry after such a long trip. Perhaps, you both would like to come to our house for supper before heading back to Star Ranch."

"I appreciate your offer, ladies." Luke nodded to the ladies before he turned back and said, "But Miss McKinley and I have a few things to discuss. We'll take supper at the Blue Bell."

Maybe she shouldn't have insisted that Mr. Griffin speak, Shannon thought. She wasn't sure she cared for his tone of voice. He most certainty sounded irritated.

However, she knew it was probably just as well that they didn't have an audience for their discussion. She sensed he wasn't exactly pleased with her. And, of course, she was certain she knew the reason.

Shannon followed him to the boardinghouse, trotting to keep up with his long strides. Mr. Griffin said nothing else until they were seated at a small table in the corner of the Blue Bell. The eating establishment was a far cry from the places where she'd eaten back home. All the tables were covered with worn, blue gingham tablecloths, but Shannon was so hungry she really didn't care.

"'Tis lovely tae sit at a real table fer a meal, Mr. Griffin," Shannon said with a smile, hoping to ease the tension crackling between them.

He didn't smile back.

Instead he took a deep breath and leaned forward, his arms propped on the table. "Let's cut straight to the point. I do believe, Miss McKinley, that I advertised for an older woman, capable of taking care of my children," Luke told her in a low voice, his stern-faced expression speaking volumes. "You are anything but old."

"I know what ye are sayin', but I'm older than I look," Shannon informed him. "I dinna believe that the advertisement stated that I had tae be an exact age. Ye need tae think o' it as gettin' more fer yer money. I'm sure ye'll find I can keep up with yer wee bairns better than someone o' a matronly age."

"You lied, Miss McKinley."

"Nae." She shook her head. "I dinna lie. Ye just see old differently than I."

He paused while the waitress placed two steaming plates of stew in front of them.

"Enjoy your stew, Luke," the woman said with a special smile. "And you be sure to save room for some of my apple pie, honey. I know how much you like it." She then looked at Shannon. "Is this your new nanny?"

"Yes, I am," Shannon said before Luke could reply.

"Welcome to Cottonwood, hon. I hope you'll enjoy your stay." The woman wasn't much older than Shannon, and she was lovely in a plump sort of way, however she looked tired and weary. But she did seem to have an interest in Mr. Griffin, Shannon noticed as the woman smiled once again at him before turning to leave. Maybe this woman could be his future wife and then he wouldn't need a nanny. Heaven forbid.

"You're not staying," Luke informed Shannon curtly. Then he picked up his fork and began to eat as if everything were decided.

"Ye dinna appear tae be an unreasonable mon," Shannon said, her accent growing thicker with her aggravation. "What does age huv tae do with carin' fer yer bairns?"

"My what?"

"Yer bairns ... wee ones."

"Children?" he clarified.

Shannon nodded and reached for her glass.

"Look at you," Luke said, pointing his fork at her.

Shannon sat back in her chair, her brow arched. She immediately set her glass back on the table to refrain from throwing the contents in his face. "And what exactly is wrong with me?"

"You're too frail. There is no meat on your bones. This land is harsh. I don't want to bury you, too."

"I dinna intend tae die, as yer poor wife did, Mr. Griffin." Shannon realized she'd made a mistake by mentioning his wife the minute Luke's expression clouded in anger. "I may be a wee bit small, but I'm sturdy and strong."

"Do not speak about my wife," Luke said. "You know nothing about her. I assume you heard gossip from the two old biddies on the stage," he snapped, his curtness lashing out at her. He didn't ask the last as a question, because he knew the answer.

Shannon could see he was a bit touchy where his late wife was concerned, but she wasn't finished. And she refused to be judged by this stubborn man.

"And ye know nothin' about me, either. Yet ye sit there

judging me by my appearance," she managed to reply through stiff lips. "I'm a Highlander. I come from a harsh land. I do admit that yer country is different, but 'tis harsh nonetheless. Where mine is green, yer country is brown and could use a few trees. We endure cold summer rains and harsh winters where yer summers are hot and dry, but I'll huv ye know I'm not the frail wee thing ye seem tae think I am, mon. And I assure ye, I'm quite capable o' takin' care o' yer bairns." She paused and took a breath. "I understand from the Millers that ye be needin' the help now, and I seem tae be the only person steppin' up."

Luke took a sip of coffee before he answered. He smiled benignly as if dealing with a temperamental child. "You'll not survive out here. I know. Like you've already been told, I buried my wife, and she was bigger than you are. You'll never make it."

Shannon placed her fork on the table. How could she penetrate his deliberate blank gaze? Looking him square in the eye, she told him, "I resent that."

Luke appeared surprised, and he drew his brows together in a frown. "What?"

"Dinna presume that I'll not survive." She shook her finger at him then brushed the loose hair that had fallen into her eyes away from her face. *Oh, but he was a stubborn one.* "And if I do die, what will it matter tae ye, mon?" She pointed out. "I'm only hired help, not yer wife. So what do ye huv tae lose?"

Though he wanted to, Luke couldn't seem to take his eyes off the woman across from him. He tried hard not to smile at her brash statement as sparks seemed to flash deep in her emerald green eyes. Even after she was gone he would never forget a single detail of her face. My God, she was lovely, or would be if she let her odd colored hair out of the severe bun she'd fashioned on top of her head. This was not the pinch-faced older woman he'd wanted to hire; nor someone he could ignore and simply go about his business.

How could anyone ignore such radiant red hair and those sparkling emerald eyes? Even now, he was fighting his own battle of personal restraint. He had to send her away. He knew he didn't want her to die. Why? He wasn't sure. Nor did he want to find out.

Luke hadn't looked twice at any woman since his wife's death. He tried to keep her memory pure. The deadness inside him would never go away, nor would his guilt or the fear that her death had been his fault. He had to admit, though, that his body had reacted the first moment he'd seen Miss McKinley. Where the admission came from, he didn't know. It seemed to have been dredged from a place beyond logic and reason. But it was nothing, he told himself. The woman had to go.

"Have you finished your meal?" Luke asked abruptly.

"'Twas delicious," Shannon said as she daintily dabbed at her mouth with a cloth. "Thank ye."

Luke wiped his mouth, tossed his napkin on the table and stood. "Let's go." He picked up his black hat.

Shannon wanted to smile. He was going to let her stay. She could feel it. But she thought better than to show a smug smile.

They left the Blue Bell and started back toward the post office, a two-story frame building on the southeast corner of town. They paused twice as the townsfolk stopped them to greet Mr. Griffin. Shannon waited patiently, wondering why they were returning to the post office, and why he wasn't taking the time to introduce her to the people of the town. Perhaps he'd forgotten to get all his mail.

When they were moving again, she asked, "How far is your ranch?"

"Five miles out of town. But I'm afraid you won't be seeing it, because I'm sending you right back to where you came from."

Shannon felt her cheeks burn hot, and she was sure they had turned bright red. Her voice trembled with indignation when she said, "Ye brought me all the way out here just tae send me back? Yer a pig-headed fool, mon."

Luke threw back his head and laughed. "That, I don't deny, but you're still going back home. I'll not have you die on me."

"For God's sake, mon. I'm not gonna die!"

Luke opened the post office door, leaving her alone on the boardwalk. But she was smart enough to stand close enough so she could hear and see what was being said.

"Where is Shorty?"

A heavyset man from behind the counter looked up. "He's already gone. Said he was running behind and had to make up time."

"Shit!" Luke swore then spun on his heel to leave.

Smiling, Shannon managed to move away from the door so he wouldn't know that she was eavesdropping. He marched through the doorway, letting the screen door slam behind him. For a moment, he just stared across the street, his hands on his hips. Finally he swung around to face her. Again he didn't speak. It appeared to her that he was trying to control his temper.

"Now what?" she asked innocently.

"It seems, Miss McKinley . . ." He took a deep breath. "Shorty has already left. Appears I have no choice, but to keep you since I can't leave you in town unescorted until the stage returns. I guess you are my responsibility so you have a job for thirty days. Maybe by then I'll have found another nanny. Until then, you can work for your keep."

Shannon smiled triumphantly, lifted her chin and boldly met his gaze. "I'll try not tae die on ye in the next month."

She noticed a small smile quirk his lips, but he quickly turned away from her. He might be a stubborn, but so was she.

"Quit gloating and come on. Time's a wasting," Luke said, taking her arm and ushering her along the boardwalk. Not bothering to stop, he added, "You haven't met my children yet. You could be running for the stage when the time comes."

ALASDAIR AND CALLUM MCKINLEY arrived in Cottonwood three hours behind the stagecoach carrying Shannon and the Miller sisters. Both were covered in the white trail dust.

"Are ye sure this is the town Shannon came tae?" Alasdair asked, a note of doubt in his voice.

Callum pulled down the red handkerchief covering his mouth. "Aye, the mon at the last depot described a young lass with hair like the setting sun boarding the stage fer Cottonwood."

"Why in God's name she'd want tae live in this brown, dusty place is beyond me, especially when she could have the rollin' green hills of Scotland."

"She deserted her clan," Callum said, then added, "Ye must not be forgettin' that Angus promised that she would marry Buchanan. Now he looks foolish that his daughter up and ran away."

"I have not forgettin'," Alasdair said. "We must find her and take her home."

"Then we better start lookin' around and see what information we can find. We won't get much done by standin' around and the sooner we can leave this God forsaken place, the better."

"Hopefully the lass will see reason and come home peacefully," Alasdair said.

"Aye, but if not, she will huv tae be persuaded one way or the other."

3

*S*hannon walked with Mr. Griffin toward a wagon. She noticed a man dressed similarly to her boss standing near the back. Reddish brown hair and blue eyes, the stranger was several inches shorter than Mr. Griffin and had a warm, friendly smile.

"This is Wilson, my foreman at the ranch," Luke said.

"Ma'am," Wilson touched a finger to the brim of his hat before favoring her with another smile. She noticed he had a bandage on his arm and wondered if he'd been involved in the shootout too.

"Mr. Wilson," Shannon said.

"Just Wilson," Luke corrected, handling her up onto the seat.

Shannon had thought that riding in a mail coach had been bad, until she climbed upon the conveyance Mr. Griffin called a buckboard. She thought the name certainly appropriate since the seat was little more than a rough, hard board nailed to the front of a crude wagon.

Both men loaded the two trunks on the buckboard while Shannon watched, impressed by their strength. When they were ready to go, she placed her valise under the hard board where she sat.

Climbing up beside her, Luke took the reins in his gloved hands then sent Wilson ahead on horseback to *warn* everyone that she was coming, as he'd put it. Shannon wasn't too sure what that meant since the houses she'd seen so far didn't require a staff like Uncle Montgomery had, and there would likely be no grand homes in the wilds of Texas, anyway. Would she be the only civilized person on Mr. Griffin's ranch?

They hadn't been riding very long before Shannon realized that Luke wasn't the example of a witty conversationalist. Thirty minutes passed in dead silence as she turned her attention to the passing landscape of barren land.

Mr. Griffin had propped his left boot on a running board, and his elbow rested on his leg as he held the reins between gloved fingers and stared straight ahead. Even in his relaxed posture, his confidence was apparent in the way he expertly drove the team of horses, but if he remembered she was there, he didn't acknowledge the fact. He was nothing like the English gentlemen who'd crowded around her vying for her attention. She tried not to be offended but still ...

In spite of his rudeness, Shannon really couldn't imagine that his children could possibly be as bad as he'd let on. More likely he was trying to frighten her away. And he had made it abundantly clear he didn't want her to stay. *She was too frail to live and work on his ranch.* Well, she'd prove him wrong, she mused, chancing a glance at him from beneath her lowered lashes.

His firm chin spoke of his stubbornness, not that she needed something else to remind her of that. He'd demonstrated his hard-headedness very clearly with his unwillingness to see reason. However, what he lacked in manners, he made up for in appearance. His tanned, rugged face spoke of his love for the outdoors, and she couldn't help wondering if the tan faded in the winter months. She would find out for herself, assuming she was still with the family when winter came.

There was something compelling about him, she had to admit. His eyes were most expressive, but he shielded his emotions. She suspected he kept many secrets hidden deep in his soul, secrets he didn't care to share with anyone. She wasn't sure she'd ever met anyone like him. He seemed very direct, yet she sensed he held something back.

She fervently hoped he would change his mind about her.

She needed this position. Considering the wide-open spaces they were passing through, she was certain her father would not be likely to find her out here.

After an hour, Shannon finally asked with a wry smile, "Do ye normally talk this much?" Even arguing would be better than this silence while they traveled.

Luke Griffin turned and glanced at her, a slow smile reluctantly brushing his lips. "Pretty much."

She really didn't need to be looking at his lips, Shannon told herself sternly. Full, with a hint of softness, they were much too inviting and caused her to wonder how well he kissed. Not that she'd likely find out. She was there to be his nanny, not his paramour. But still . . . "Huv ye had many gunfights like the one I saw?"

"Too many," he answered grimly. When it appeared he wasn't going to explain further, Shannon decided she'd have to drag it out of him. But to her surprise, he said, "Sorry you had to see that fight back in town."

"I've seen men fightin' before in Scotland, but never

quite like that. They're more likely tae be shoutin' that they're gettin' ready tae kill each other. Their method o' fightin' is broadswords and bare hands."

"I think I prefer our way a little better," Luke commented wryly.

Shannon looked at him for a moment, startled at his attempt at humor. If that was supposed to be humor, she didn't quite know how to respond. "Is there some kind o' authority here in Cottonwood or a laird who controls the town?"

"Laird?"

"One mon who makes all the rules. The one all the others report tae."

"Most towns have a sheriff, but Cottonwood doesn't have one at the moment. Afraid there isn't much law in Texas Territory. Mostly, we protect and safeguard our property any way we see fit. The worst crime is horse-stealing."

Shannon's mouth dropped open. "Even more than killing a mon?"

"Yep."

She saw a devilish spark in Luke's eyes that made him appear boyish. Evidently, he was amused that horses were more valuable than living men. In spite of that thought, she liked his wry humor. Perhaps, Mr. Griffin took pleasure in her company even if he didn't want to admit it.

Despite his earlier silence, Shannon most certainly enjoyed his company, especially the way his solid form brushed against her every time the wagon rolled through a rut in the road, which was very peculiar since she normally didn't like men touching her at all. She'd had enough of her father grabbing her. Yet she enjoyed watching Mr. Griffin's strong hands grip the reins, his long legs shifting as he guided the horses. She felt comfortable with him even if he was a perfect stranger.

"Ye mean everyone values a horse's life higher than that o' a mon?"

Mr. Griffin shoved his hat back a little so he could look at her. His green eyes sparkled. "Yep. Know how it sounds, but a man without a horse is pretty much a dead man out here."

"So did ye steal the mon's horse? Is that what ye were fightin' aboot?"

"What man?" Luke glanced at her as if she were completely daft.

"The mon ye shot." Shannon couldn't understand why he couldn't keep up with the conversation. "Is that what ye were fightin' aboot?"

"Nope." Luke shook his head and let out an impatient sigh. "He was a hothead looking to make a reputation for himself as a gunslinger, Thought he could add a notch to his belt by shooting me."

"I dinna ken."

"Beg your pardon," he looked at her. "Ken?"

"Aye, ken," she paused. "Understand."

"He was a man who liked to kill and then brag about how many men he'd killed. The more important the victim, the bigger the man feels."

Shannon thought that over for a moment. These men killed for fun. How barbaric! And she'd thought America was civilized. Now she wondered. "So yer important?"

He chuckled. "I guess you could say I used to be."

"Well I'm glad he dinna kill ye."

"Me too," Luke grinned, studying her from beneath the brim of his hat. The woman really was like a breath of fresh air with her obvious understatement. And with her trim figure and that glorious red hair, she'd primly pinned up beneath her hat, no doubt his ranch hands would flock to her side and bend over backwards to please her. He frowned at the thought as the wagon hit another rut in the road. Shannon's curves brushed against him, soft, pliant. He shuddered. After all, he did still have red blood in his veins. He hadn't missed the way his body had reacted to her.

Would her hair tumble to her hips when he loosened it from those confounding pins? He wondered as he watched strands of hair blow freely around her face. He sighed as a pang of guilt hit him. He knew there was no reason to feel guilty about noticing a beautiful young woman. His wife had been dead for two long years, but the guilt was there just the same.

It wasn't only Shannon's appearance that had caught his eye -- there was confidence in the way she moved that interested him. For a little thing, she had plenty of fire, just like the glint of her hair. And Luke found that a part of him that had been dead for a long time could still be aroused.

He should have left her back in town, Luke told himself as he tried to keep his attention on the poor excuse for a road. He sensed this nanny would be trouble. But his children needed someone who could lead them along the right path.

Was this . . . girl the one who could do it?

He sure had failed them once Ruth had fallen sick. He'd all but forgotten about the children, as his whole focus had been on his wife. He shook his head. They needed a woman in their lives: someone to teach them what he couldn't. Oh, he wanted to be closer to his children, but frankly he didn't know how. And with a spread as big as his, there was always so much to do. Too much.

Too bad this woman wasn't what he'd had in mind.

What he'd asked for. He needed a stern, sturdy spinster to handle his unruly children. Those rascals would chase this elf of a woman off in no time, and then he'd be right back where he'd started.

"How far is yer ranch?" Shannon asked, wondering what kind of home he had. She couldn't imagine him living in any of the small, low wooden buildings like the ones she'd seen so far. He'd have to duck to enter most doorways. Mr. Griffin seemed the kind to have the best, no matter how hard he had to work for it. But did that make sense way out here in the middle of nowhere?

"About another mile."

Shannon was about to comment on his curt sentences, when something scurried across the road in front of them. The horses reared, jolting the wagon.

Shannon screamed as she was thrown toward Mr. Griffin, landing in his lap. "By the saints above, 'tis a wild beast!"

The wagon bucked as Luke struggled to hold the woman who was now in his lap. He pulled back on the reins to steady the horses too frightened to obey his commands. "Whoa, whoa!" he shouted both to the horses and to Shannon. For a split-second, he couldn't help thinking how good she felt, so soft and small against his large hard body, but first things first.

Gaining control of the horses, he slipped the leather straps to one hand and gently lifted her off him and back onto her side of the seat, but with a pang of regret. "See. You have proven my point. If you go getting scared over a little armadillo, you're not going to make it out here."

She straightened her skirt with a flourish. Her cheeks were a lovely shade of pink. "Arma . . . 'Twas a rat in armor!"

Luke chuckled. "I take it they don't have armadillos in your part of the world?"

"Nay. I've never seen such a thing."

"You'll probably see many creatures here you haven't seen before."

"Such as yerself?" Shannon teased.

"Yep." Luke clucked his tongue and the horses started forward, obeying his simple command like they were trained to do. That's what he liked, everything in order. Luke glanced at his companion, thinking she'd never take orders from anyone she really didn't want to. "Tell me. What is it like where you come from?"

"I've lived the last three years in England, but I was born in Scotland. 'Tis beautiful there: lush, green all the time from plenty of cool rains."

"Well, you probably won't see lush and green here until next spring. But then you're only staying a month, so it won't get too cold before you're on your way."

"Aye, a month," Shannon said with a rueful smile. The mon needed her -- he just didn't know how much he needed her -- yet. "'Tis verra dry here. Does it never rain?"

"Actually, it rains a little more here than other parts of Texas that are very dry. I built my house near a river so you'll see plenty of water, if you're worried about shriveling up like a dead leaf," he said with a slight smile, and she realized he was actually teasing her.

"'Tis good tae know. I think one feels better when they are around water."

"Since you'll be caring for my children, I suppose I should know a little about you. What did your family say about you traveling so far from home?"

"'Tis complicated, I fear," she said with a sigh before averting her gaze.

She was avoiding the question. That wasn't a good sign, Luke thought. "Indulge me."

Shannon cut her eyes to him. My, she thought, the mon was persistent. Then a tinge of guilt hit her. Perhaps he did have a right to know a little about her past. She didn't have to tell him the entire story. "Well, my mother died aboot five years ago now. My da -- let's just say he's not a nice mon."

"So you came over all by yourself?"

"Nay. I huv a cousin and a friend who are like sisters tae me. Jocelyn stayed in New York tae pursue whatever 'tis she wants tae do. Sounds odd, but she's a bit fickle, so it might take her a long while tae make up her mind. And Brooke, she inherited a plantation near New Orleans."

Luke regarded her for a moment. She wondered what he was thinking.

"Why in the world didn't you go to New Orleans with your friend or should I say sister? It's a little more settled there than Texas."

"I wanted tae be on my own," Shannon explained, stubbornly. "I've been fascinated with the west and everything that I've read aboot in books. We dinna get many books aboot the west in my country, but enough tae get my curiosity up.

"I also love children, so I thought yer situation was perfect fer me. I dinna know much aboot where ye live, but I like adventure, and so far I've not been disappointed. Do ye huv any family, Mr. Griffin? Besides the children."

"Look," Luke paused then glanced at her. "I don't really like formalities. Texas isn't very formal or civilized as I'm sure you've noticed so why don't you call me Luke, and I'll call you Shannon. Makes things simple."

Shannon gave a nod and said softly, "Luke." His given name felt strange on her tongue. She wasn't accustomed to being so familiar with a man she barely knew, but then she was traveling alone across great distances of the wilderness with him, she realized, so what did a name matter?

Luke grunted at the sound of his name on her lips as a thrilling current rippled through him. It was downright irritating. It was the first time he'd felt anything like it in a long time and along with the excitement came the guilt. He didn't know whether to enjoy it or curse it, nor did he know how to stop feeling guilty.

His wife had meant everything to him. When she'd smiled, his world had been complete. He wasn't certain he would ever find that in another woman. Not that he'd been looking, mind you.

Luke had to admit, though, that Ruth had always been frail, taking to her bed with every excuse. She'd never liked Texas as he had. Why hadn't he taken her back to Boston long before she'd come down with that fever?

With the guilty question rolling around his head, he didn't hear the woman beside him.

"Perhaps, I shouldn't call ye by yer given name if it's goin' tae make ye frown."

Luke blinked to clear his thoughts, then turned to her. Thank goodness he could see the two wagon wheels marking the entrance to Star Ranch ahead in the distance. Something about Shannon disturbed him. "The ranch is up ahead," he grumbled.

Shannon couldn't see anything as the buckboard swung onto the road leading under an archway of two wagon wheels. The ranch was as mysterious as the man who looked so hopeless and empty. He'd been carrying on a normal conversation with her a minute ago, and now he'd gone back to his brooding. What had she done to cause the change in him?

They traveled another quarter of a mile until they

suddenly topped a hill. She hadn't realized they had been climbing until Luke drew the wagon to a halt. The view below caused her to gasp with surprise and fascination as she stared down.

There in the valley sat a large house, shaded by trees of a variety she didn't recognize. A river ran behind the house, providing the water necessary to maintain such large trees and making this small piece of land seem like paradise compared to what she'd seen of Texas so far.

The ranch house was quite different than the grand English manor she'd been in. Instead of being several stories high, this one was long and low to the ground. And it was of a strange material, painted white outside instead of being made of brick or wood.

"Yer home is quite lovely," Shannon said, filled with awe she couldn't hide. "I dinna believe I've ever seen a house with such a different construction."

"It's made of adobe. Sun-dried mud bricks," he explained. "Then it's whitewashed so that it reflects the heat. Very helpful in the summer when the sun is blistering hot." Luke smiled and Shannon thought it was something he should do more often.

"I'll admit it's a bit fancier than most folks have around here, but Ruth was from Boston. She wouldn't have lived in a shack, therefore the Victorian wood trim. I'm sure it's different from the kinds of places you've lived in, but I think you'll enjoy the roominess. Even though it is a single structure, there are two wings arranged in a U-shape."

"'Tis much larger than I would huv thought."

"Nine rooms."

"'Tis grand, indeed. Ye've done a good job with yer home. I know ye must be verra proud," Shannon said, her voice full of praise.

Luke's chest swelled with pride. He appreciated the fact that Shannon liked his home, and she didn't seem to mind that the nearest neighbor was miles away. Ruth had complained about the isolation. However the biggest test was still ahead of Shannon. How well she'd get along with his children might be an entirely different story.

Luke didn't have much time to wonder because as soon as he drew the horses to a halt and the wagon stopped, his children came barreling around the house. They were covered head to toe with dirt.

Shannon watched Luke's two small children come to a tumbling halt. As soon as they were still, they stared at her, their big, bright eyes filled with questions. She needed to get off this infernal contraption and meet the children closer to their level, but she didn't want to fall flat on her face and look the fool, so she waited until Luke offered to help her down.

She accepted with a nod and turned toward him. He lifted her to the ground as easily as if she were a feather. Shannon had to admit she liked his support and the feel of his strong hands grasping her waist longer than necessary. She glanced up and caught a fleeting expression of some unnamed emotion in his gaze before he quickly masked his face again and dropped his hands to his sides.

Shannon turned to the children. *Oh my*, she thought. The only way she could tell one of them was a girl was because she had her hair bound in long pigtails. Shannon thought the child's hair was blonde, but she was none too sure at the moment because it was so dirty.

"Huv ye been playin' with the pigs?" she asked them.

"Yes, we have," they both said.

"They are a sight, I agree, and I do apologize," Luke said, though his voice held little remorse. Then he addressed his children. "I told you two not to get into any trouble."

"We've just been playing, Pa," the smallest, presumably the youngest, said and added, "The pig had babies." He pointed a grimy little finger toward Shannon. "Who's she?"

Luke reached for Shannon's elbow. "Children, I'd like for you to meet Miss McKinley, your new nanny."

"Aw, Pa. We don't want no nanny," they said in unison.

"So you've told me in the past," Luke commented ruefully, more for Shannon than the children's benefit.

The little girl added, "She talks funny."

"Ye think so," Shannon said with a smile. "And I thought ye were the ones who sounded funny."

"Miss McKinley, these are my children. Molly is eight and Toby six."

"Hello, children," Shannon said, stooping down to their level and gravely offering her hand. "I'm sure we'll get along famously."

Neither child responded.

Shannon could tell right away the children were going to be a handful. The stubbornness she saw on their faces told her she'd have to be strict. They certainly took after their father in that regard.

"I can see we'll huv a period o' adjustment. However, there's no time like the present tae start. I dinna want tae make this any more painful than I huv to," she said firmly. "Now let's get ye both bathed before dinner."

Molly took a step back. "Don't want no bath," she said sulkily.

Shannon rose and brushed the dirt off her hand. "Come along," she said as she turned towards the steps to the front door.

"What's she mean by painful?" Toby asked his sister.

"I'm not sure," Molly said then glanced at her father. "Do we have to wash up now?"

"Yes, Molly." Luke scooped them both up into his arms and carried them to the house. "Miss McKinley is in charge. You'll do as she says," he said firmly.

Shannon paused by the door, waiting for Luke and the children to join her. "I prefer that the children call me Miss Shannon, if that is all right with ye." She noticed he hadn't told the children she was only staying thirty days.

Luke stopped in front of her. "Whatever you wish, Miss McKinley."

"Ye can call me Shannon, too. As ye said before, ye dinna like formalities way out here."

Luke nodded then seemed a little puzzled. "Are you waiting for something?"

"Aye. Have ye forgotten yer manners? A gentleman should always open a door fer a lady. Besides which, 'tisn't my house, and ye haven't invited me in." Shannon looked up at Luke and she could swear that the man blushed.

"S'pose I'm a little rusty," Luke muttered. "Don't get much company out here." He set the children down and opened the door for her.

The children tried to dart in front of her, something she'd anticipated. Shannon snagged them both by the arm and held them back. "Children, I believe ye need tae learn a few manners, and there is no time like the present tae start. Ye dinna dart in front o' grownups, and ladies always go first. Do ye ken?"

"Ken?" the children repeated like parrots.

"Understand." Evidently not, she sighed, because both children stared at her as though she were speaking in tongues.

"Toby, stand over beside your father. I will enter first and then Molly wull follow since she is a lady in disguise."

Molly grinned at that bit of news, then turned and stuck her tongue out at her brother.

"Toby, ye wull follow yer sister. Understood?"

Luke never realized that going through the front door could be such a pain in the ass. He still needed to ride out to the range before dinner and see if the boys had finished putting up the fence, and this nonsense was wasting valuable time.

However, as the woman swept by him, he had to admit she did have a point. He had forgotten so much about civilized living since Ruth had been gone. So had his children. They'd grown wild in the absence of a woman at the ranch, and in his neglect. Not only had he failed them he'd failed Ruth, too.

As he watched the children march into the house, Luke resisted the urge to smile. He'd love to stay and watch Miss McKinley struggle with the children's baths, but he had chores to do. Besides, giving each a bath required more muscle than roping a calf, but would be a lot more entertaining to watch, he wagered.

"Cook," he called out as he followed them inside.

Shortly, a woman appeared from the back of the house and Shannon turned toward her. The woman was a brown-skinned lady who looked to be in her thirties.

"This is Shannon McKinley. She is the children's new nanny." He turned to Shannon. "Shannon McKinley, this is our wonderful cook and jack of all trades who I simply call Cook. She makes the best refried beans in all of Texas."

"'Tis nice tae meet ye." Shannon extended her hand, wanting to ask the woman why she had to recook beans, but that could wait until later. There were more important things at hand. "I can unpack later if ye just show me where tae bathe the children."

"You're going to wash them by yourself, Señorita?"

"Aye."

The children had other ideas as they tried to dash out the door, but Shannon caught them by the backs of their shirts. "Now, ye really were not thinkin' aboot runnin' off, were ye?"

Luke chuckled. "You children behave. And don't give Miss Shannon a hard time," he said, his expression changing to a sterner one. Amazing how easy her name rolled off his tongue. "It's been a while since you've had a spanking, and you don't want to end the day with one, do you?"

Both children shook their heads.

"Good. Since we have an understanding, I'll get some work done and see you at dinner." Luke told them and left the house. As he strode to the barn, he wondered what the three of them would look like over dinner. Would the children still be dirty and Shannon soaked? He chuckled as he thought about it. Maybe that would be enough to make her ready to go back to town.

Reckoned he'd find out tonight. And damn if he didn't look forward to having dinner with all of them. Strange, it had been a long time since he'd looked forward to anything, and he suspected that Miss McKinley was the cause.

4

———

*S*hannon didn't bother to take a grand tour of the house nor ask where her room was located. After all, she wasn't a guest and could learn the layout of the house later. She needed to prove to Luke that she was perfectly capable of taking care of his children.

At the moment, she had one goal in mind, and that was to bathe those filthy children.

Shannon turned to the woman who Luke had called Cook. "If ye'll show me where the children can be bathed and provide us with some hot water, I'd be most grateful."

"I ain't grateful," Toby grumbled.

"Ye are not grateful," Shannon corrected.

Toby twisted his head up to look at her. "Yeah, that's what I said."

"But ye dinna say it correctly," Shannon gently pointed out. "I see we'll huv a great deal o' work tae do." She nodded toward the hallway. "Lead the way, if you please."

Shannon heard Toby whisper to his sister, "She sure talks funny," as they trudged down the hall trailing their grubby fingers along the wall.

The housekeeper motioned to Shannon. "We have bathing rooms, señorita, specially built on both wings of the house. Everything you'll need will be in there, and I'll find some clean clothes for the *niños* and place them on their beds," she said with a smile. "Their rooms are next to the bathing room."

"*Niños?*"

"*Sí--* children," the woman explained.

"We call them *bairns*," Shannon said.

The housekeeper was a middle-aged, Mexican woman with brown skin, dark hair, and warm eyes the color of chocolate. She was dressed in a bright orange and red striped dress, which complimented her skin perfectly. Shannon found that she liked the gentle woman with her easy smile.

"I do appreciate yer help," She told her. "Surely, ye huv a name other than cook?"

"*Sí, señorita*. My name is Maria. Señor Luke was being funny calling me cook."

"What a lovely name," Shannon said with a smile. "Are ye from the Texas Territory?"

"*Sí*. We move here from Mexico when I was much younger. So this feels like home."

"I'm sorry tae be so much trouble, but I'm sure I'll be needin' yer help until I've learned my way around here."

The children who had reached the bathing room darted inside. *Hopefully, there is no outside escape door*, Shannon thought wryly. She'd hate to have to run them down again.

"If you can harness those two," Maria said, nodding toward the children, "then you're a good one, *señorita*. They have been allowed to run wild far too long. You're the sixth nanny they have had."

"Why so many?"

"The others said the money wasn't worth putting up with such ill-mannered *niños*," Maria answered as they followed the children down the hallway. "Our third nanny lasted the longest. A full five days before she ran off." Maria glanced at her out of the corner of her eye, looking extremely guilty.

Shannon stopped and peered at Maria. "You're not tellin' me somethin'."

"*Sí.*" Maria's dark eyebrows slanted in a frown. "I--I hate to tell you, but the men are already making wagers on how long you'll stay." She paused and shrugged. "An--and I am afraid I made a little wager, too."

Shannon laughed. "If ye want tae make some money, bet fer the longest time," she suggested. "I grew up in the wilds of Scotland, so I'm a strappin' lass, and a bit o' hard work willna frighten me away." Pausing, Shannon reached for the doorknob. "Now, I need tae scrub these two *bairns*."

Maria nodded and gave her a warm, good luck smile before leaving her.

When Shannon entered the room she found it spacious, with white walls and potted green plants. Two large tubs, complete with claw feet like the kind she had back home, sat in the center of the room. A partition between them provided a nice touch and plenty of privacy for each child.

Without warning, a vision of herself in one tub and Luke in the other flashed across her mind. Just as quickly, she shoved that particular image to the back of her mind, unsure of where it had come from.

Two maids were already filling the tubs with hot water. The steam rolled up in the air, looking very inviting. Shannon wouldn't mind a bath herself. It had been a long journey, but that small luxury had to wait.

Evidently, Mr. Griffin had already given instructions for

baths because the tubs were nearly full. When the maids had finished, they waited for Shannon to dismiss them, then exited through a back door leading to the outdoors. No wonder the children hadn't darted outside to freedom when they had the chance.

Shannon rolled up her sleeves and turned to Toby and Molly who were standing near the door, their arms folded belligerently over their skinny chests, ready to escape if an opportunity presented itself. "The one thing I canna abide is filthy lads and lassies. A little dirt isn't a problem, but the two o' ye go far beyond that. Toby, ye go over tae that tub behind the screen, strip down and climb into the tub."

"I don't want to," Toby declared, slumping to the floor with his arms crossed over his chest.

Shannon raised her brow at the stubborn child, knowing his sister would follow suit. Quickly, she strode over to both doors and locked them, putting the keys in her pocket.

"Hey, whatcha doing?" Molly demanded, alarm evident in her tone.

"We're not leavin' this room until yer skin is scrubbed clean and pink. Now --" Shannon took a deep, controlled breath and crossed her arms over her chest. "Ye can bathe while the water is hot or ye can wait until it turns cold. Makes no difference tae me. Either way, yer takin' a bath."

Neither of the children moved.

Undaunted, Shannon smiled slowly at them. They didn't realize just how stubborn she could be, too, and she'd had many years of practice. "Perhaps, I need tae be helpin' ye take yer clothes off," she said airily, directing her attention towards Toby. "I thought ye'd be old enough tae undress by yerselves," she said, shrugging. "But I see yer still babies that need my help."

Toby scrunched his face, narrowing his eyes, and glared at her. "I ain't no baby," he stated stubbornly. However, he did grudgingly scramble to his feet, then stomped off behind the screen.

"He is too a baby," Molly declared, sticking her tongue out in Toby's direction. But she too had begun to undress.

"I'm not," Toby shouted back.

"Are too! 'Cause I'm the oldest."

Shannon grabbed an apron that was draped over a chair and slipped it over her head. Wonderful. They were communicating even if it was in the form of shouting.

The saints above must be testing me. Shannon couldn't help thinking.

She tied the generous, white apron in the back and prepared to supervise. "Ye know, bein' the oldest carries many responsibilities," she told Molly matter-of-factly.

Molly had just finished removing her underclothes. Next she stepped up on the small stool and slid down into the warm water that covered her to her chin.

Shannon knelt beside the tub and prepared to scrub. She smiled as she noted how the child appeared so small in the huge vessel of water. She picked up a washrag and a bar of soap and lathered it up to show Molly how to do it. "With ye bein' the oldest, yer younger brother will always look up tae ye fer advice." She dipped the washrag up and down in the water to rinse out the excess suds. "Shut yer eyes," Shannon instructed, then she soaped the rag again and scrubbed the child's face, watching with keen interest as layer after layer of dirt slid off. Molly spit out the soap in protest as Shannon poured water over her head. "My, my, there is a bonny lass under all that dirt."

"A bonny lass?"

"In my country, a girl is called a lass and a lad is a boy.

And bonny means pretty."

"Uh huh," Molly said as if she heard the explanation every day, then she went on with what was important to her and whispered, "I like telling Toby what to do."

"I imagine ye do." Shannon smiled. "'Tis an advantage o' bein' older. Ye get tae experience everythin' first."

"I can hear you talking about me," Toby shouted from the other side of the partition. "I'm clean."

"I doubt that," Shannon replied.

"Well, I'm tired of sitting in here."

Shannon couldn't help laughing. "I'll get tae ye as soon as I wash yer sister's hair."

"Molly, I'm going tae huv a time gettin' these tangles out of yer hair. I'll try not tae pull yer hair, but with these knots, it'll be a job not tae hurt ye some." After several minutes, the dirty blonde hair hung loose and smooth over the girl's shoulders.

Shannon reached for the grubby ribbons that had fallen from Molly's hair and were floating in the water. The child turned and snatched the ribbons from Shannon's hand. "They're mine!"

Shannon studied the rebellious child with a raised brow. "Ye huv the manners of a pig." She sighed deeply. She was going to have a lot of work ahead of her. "Yes, they are yers," she acknowledged calmly. "But the next time, ask first before jerkin' anything out o' my hand, ye ken?"

When Molly didn't answer, Shannon repeated, "Ye ken?"

"My mother gave them to me," Molly said in a softer voice.

Shannon offered her a forgiving smile. "Then they must be verra special tae ye," she said solemnly. "But I think yer mother would be verra disappointed in yer manners," Shannon told her. It was obvious that the child was trying hard not to cry by the way her small, lower lip wobbled. "Why don't ye wash these lovely ribbons with soap while I wash yer brother. That way they wull be pretty and fresh fer tomorrow."

"I'm tired of waiting," Toby called out impatiently. "I'm all clean."

Shannon laughed at that. It would take more than a quick soak for the many layers of dirt to come off that lad. "As dirty as ye were, a good soakin' will do ye good," she shouted over the partition. "Why don't' ye be thinkin' of a good story for bedtime."

"You know how to tell stories?"

"Aye, I do."

"Oh, boy," Toby said.

As Shannon finished with Molly's hair, she thought Toby might be easier to win over than Molly. The girl was older and, therefore, more cautious, and there was no doubt that she had stronger memories of her mother. It was going to take a great deal of work with both of them. Shannon prayed her patience held.

Once she had Molly bundled in a bath sheet, Shannon said, "Go to yer room and get dressed in yer clean clothes while I take care o' this dirty lad. I'll come and help ye dry yer hair when I'm finished."

Shannon was surprised when Molly nodded instead of arguing. 'Twas good that she'd done that much, and Shannon would accept any small step as progress.

One down, one to go, she told herself, then turned her attention to Toby. He looked a lot like his father -- the same stubborn chin and green eyes -- albeit a lot dirtier. But Toby was young, so there might be time to instill some redeeming qualities into the lad before he turned into another version of his father.

To preserve his modesty, Shannon allowed Toby to wash himself. Under her supervision, of course. However, he neglected his face altogether, and she had to take over and finish the job. There was a cute little boy under all that dirt. He even had freckles.

After she sent Toby to his room to dress, Shannon checked on Molly. Shannon stood at the door and watched the child who was placing her ribbons with tender care on the windowsill to dry. A lump formed in Shannon's throat. The child must really miss her mother, and she knew all too well how that felt. The hurt never stopped.

Molly had dressed in a lovely pink gingham dress which transformed her from the street urchin she'd first seen. "Ye look quite lovely, Miss Molly," Shannon said.

Molly flashed an appreciative smile.

Shannon found a stool in the corner and placed it in front of the overstuffed chair, then settled on the dark rose-colored cushion. "Ahh," she sighed heavily, not realizing until this moment how tired she was now that she had finally slowed down. Her back ached as did her legs, and her eyes wanted nothing more than to close. Nevertheless, the children still required her attention. "Come," she said, patting the seat of the stool. "Sit here and I'll dry yer hair."

Molly obeyed, quickly settling on the footstool. Shannon picked up the discarded towel from the floor and towel-dried the child's soft blonde hair while she hummed a tune that her own mother had always sung to her when she was a child.

Reaching for the brush, Shannon said. "Ye huv such lovely hair. I'll wager 'tis like yer mother's."

"Mama had pretty hair," Molly said. "It was very long."

"Would ye like tae huv some curls in yer hair?"

Molly jerked away from Shannon, giving her a peculiar glare before she spat, "You're not my mother!"

Shannon took a deep, calming breath. Evidently, the child had felt her guard slipping away and didn't know how to handle the fact that she could accept kindness from another woman. Remembering she had done the same in her youth, Shannon let Molly's outburst slide this once, feeling her heart lurch toward the sad, defiant little girl who desperately needed someone to love her.

"Nay, I'm not yer mother," she said patiently, pulling Molly back so she could finish her hair. Shannon parted the blonde hair down the middle, then continued pulling the brush through the silky strands. "No one can ever take the place of yer mother, Molly. And I wouldna even try, but I hope that one day we might be friends."

Molly didn't respond, and Shannon didn't push. She could understand the child's confusion and resistance, but the sad fact was Molly's mother wasn't coming back, no matter how badly she wanted her to.

Shannon finished pulling Molly's hair up into pigtails. Brushing her hands off on her apron, Shannon got up and looked Molly over. "Ye are all done. And ye look verra pretty, I might add."

With a long sigh, Shannon placed her hands in the small of her back and stretched. She noticed that Molly didn't thank her, but Shannon was too weary to deal with anything other than bathing the children right now. Etiquette lessons could wait until tomorrow after she had a good night's sleep.

Her long journey weighed heavy on her shoulders, and she grew more fatigued with each passing moment. "I think I'm goin' tae lie down fer a wee bit before dinner," she said to no one in particular. "It has been a verra long day."

Molly, who had been looking at herself in the mirror, spun around. "I'll take you to your room," she volunteered, which surprised Shannon. Then again, perhaps, the child was bending just a little.

Shannon nodded and followed Molly out into the hallway, practically running over Toby in the process.

"Where you goin'?" Toby demanded.

"I'm taking Miss Shannon to her room in the *other* wing," Molly said.

"But --" Toby started, until his sister cut him off.

"Why don't you get Miss Shannon's carpetbag so she won't have to carry it."

"Sure," Toby agreed with a grin, then darted off toward the parlor.

"That's nice of Toby," Shannon murmured, covering a yawn with her hand as she walked beside Molly across the main room. "There's my carpetbag. I'm sure yer father wull have someone deliver my trunks."

They hurried into the other wing. Something about the children's eagerness bothered Shannon, but she was so tired she couldn't think clearly. It was as if the stress of the entire journey had come pounding down upon her all at once.

When they reached the end of the second hall, Molly opened the door to a magnificent room much like her own room back home in England. However, there were no feminine accents anywhere to be seen. Of course, why should there be in a house run by a man?

"I thought my room would be much smaller," Shannon said. She yawned, placing a hand over her mouth. "Are ye sure 'tis mine?"

"Uh huh. All the bedrooms are this big," Molly assured her. "The grownups stay in this wing."

"Here's your bag," Toby said, huffing and puffing as he

dragged the carpetbag behind him. "Don't know what you got in there, but the dang thing's heavy."

Shannon laughed as she took the bag. "'Tis a wee bit heavy," she agreed. "But my trunks are worse. I'll get them after my nap," she said barely stifling another yawn. She dug down in her bag and retrieved two books. "Here are two storybooks that ye can look over." She placed her bag back on the floor. "I wull see ye children at dinner. Mind ye stay clean sae yer father can see how fine his children look."

"We will," they said, darting from the room and slamming the door behind them.

She'd have to work on instilling in them how to properly close the door later along with quite a few other things. The list seemed to be growing longer and longer by the hour. Still she smiled, thinking of the children as she set her bag in a nearby chair. The bath was probably shock enough. Better not overwork them on the first day, then they would run from her.

Shannon wished she could give the children back their mother, but since that wasn't possible, perhaps she could bring a little joy, along with discipline, to their lives. And if she were really lucky, perhaps, she could bring them closer to their father as well.

Their father.

Shannon hadn't had time to think much about him since she'd arrived. Understanding Luke Griffin was a matter that would have to wait until she had a clearer mind. She found her brush tucked away in her carpetbag and placed it on the dresser. She removed the remaining hairpins and brushed out her hair.

Now to get out of these clothes, she thought as she unfastened the buttons on her blouse. She glanced around the room. 'Twas quite lovely, in spite of its lack of feminine touches. A large four poster bed was the main focus of the room, and that bed was calling her name.

It would be heavenly to have a bath, and she longed for a nice soak in a hot tub, but her legs felt like jelly and she wasn't sure how much longer they would hold her up.

So for now, she would strip down to her chemise until she could get a nightgown from one of her trunks. Leaving her hair loose and flowing around her shoulders the way she liked it, she climbed up on the large bed, moaning with relief as she sank into the feather comforter.

After a long day, this is pure heaven.

Spotting an afghan at the end of the bed, she reached down and pulled it up over her. Then she bunched up the pillow under her head and closed her eyes.

Well, I am here, Shannon thought as she drifted off to sleep – *in a strange land with people I barely know*. Perhaps she should be afraid, but she wasn't. She felt as if she'd been sent here for a real purpose -- something other than just being nanny to two wild children -- though that made no sense to her at all. Her goal, for now, was to stay and make these strangers into a family. Hopefully she'd found her cowboy, even if he was a wee bit reluctant at the moment.

Shannon knew all too well what it was like not having a father's love, and she wanted something different for these children. No child should have to endure what she had growing up. Still, they seemed somewhat better off than she had been. Their father might be remote, but he wasn't cruel as hers had been.

Just what would the next month bring? She wondered as her eyelids drifted downward. Unfortunately, she lacked an answer for that question. Her heavy eyelids slowly closed, and she was asleep before she could finish her thought.

5

The sky had turned a dusk-colored orange as Luke finished cooling down his mare and turning her into her stall. He ambled across the yard toward the back of the house, tired and hungry. The day had been too damn long and trying on his patience. The untimely appearance of yet another greenhorn eager to prove himself a fast draw had ended with the youngster losing his life in a gunfight.

Then there was the arrival of his newest nanny. What good was that slip of a girl going to do against his two hellions was beyond him. He wasn't sure which was worse: the gunfight or the nanny.

No wonder his head hurt like hell.

Then again, Wilson needling him most of the afternoon could be the reason for his ailment. While they worked side-by-side digging postholes and splitting rails for the new fence on the north range, Wilson had commented that Luke was acting as if redheaded demons were after him. And then the fool had had the nerve to grin after his comment. His ranch hand knew Shannon would weigh heavily on his mind. He'd been there when Luke had written the missive for a nanny and knew the requirements and attributes Luke wanted for a prospective candidate to fulfill. If Luke had had the energy, he'd have wiped the smirk off his foreman's ornery face.

As Luke entered the kitchen to wash up, his scowl faded when he caught a whiff of roast beef on the air. "Smells good," he called as he went to the dry sink by the back door. A contraption Maria had insisted upon when he'd hired her. She kept her kitchen spotless, and a bucket of water and towels beside the sink to ensure the room remained to her standards.

As he splashed the cool, reviving water onto his face and hands, his thoughts went back to Wilson.

Perhaps Wilson had been right after all.

Luke did feel as if a demon were after him, and she had a Scottish accent and flaming, red hair. Wilson sure had that right. But Miss McKinley would soon learn that he meant what he said. She could only stay until the next stage. He didn't need any more problems to ride herd on.

That being said, he craned his neck toward the mouth-watering aroma. A good meal could make any man feel better as far as he was concerned. He shook the excess water from his arms and dried himself on the towel that lay next to the water bucket. Then he snagged a clean shirt from the peg and shrugged into the cool cotton.

"Good evening," Luke greeted Maria and the two maids who kept each wing of the house spotless, Ada and Carmen. "Do we still have a nanny?" he asked as he buttoned his cuffs.

They nodded in unison. "*Sí*, señor," one of them said.

"I assume everyone has placed their bets?"

"*Sí*," Maria said as she placed a large roast on a white platter. "The pot is mucho big. Have you made your wager?"

Luke peered over her shoulder at the roast. "I give her thirty days. How long did you give her?"

Maria smiled. "Six months."

"Why so long?"

"This one is different, señor. I like her."

"Really?" Luke said, not hiding his surprise. "She isn't what I wanted or advertised for."

Maria glanced up from slicing the roast. "*Sí*, but the ones who met your requirements only lasted a month. If Señorita Shannon can do the job, more the better."

"Let's just say, I'll believe it when I see it. She's much too young to handle my rascals."

"And too pretty," Maria added.

"What does that have to do with anything?"

She shrugged. "Perhaps she makes you uncomfortable."

"That's bul-- uh, nonsense," Luke shot back.

Maria looked at him for a long moment. She had worked for Señor Luke a very long time, ever since he'd built his home. He was a good man, but he'd changed so much since his wife's death, blaming himself for her passing, turning a deaf ear to his children's needs and the love they so desperately needed from him.

Guilt was a heavy burden to carry, and the sad part was that Ruth had been too frail for this country to start with, plus she didn't want to be in Texas. But she'd loved Luke, and where he went, she followed, hating the thought of being apart from him more than she did leaving behind the comforts of her childhood home. Maria knew she'd never be able to convince Señor Luke that Ruth's death hadn't been his fault. It was something he had to work out by himself.

Señorita Shannon was nothing like Ruth, of that Maria was certain. The young miss hadn't been appalled by the children's disheveled appearance, nor had she frowned upon bathing them, hinting that laborious chores and lack of comfort didn't rattle her.

Noticing Señor Luke waited for her to comment, Maria finally said, "I guess we'll have to wait and see who wins." She smiled. "Shall I serve dinner?"

Astonishment shown on Luke's face for a brief moment, but he hid it quickly. "I'm heading to the dining room now. Where are the children?"

"I called them a few minutes ago. They should be in their seats waiting for you."

Luke made his way to the dining room expecting to see a frazzled nanny and children who looked pretty much the same as when he'd left. Maybe a little cleaner, God willing, and nothing more. However, when he entered the room, he had to stop a moment and stare. He wasn't even sure he was in the right house.

Swallowing back his surprise, he joshed, "What did you do with my children?" He resumed his stride toward the table. They were clean and, better yet, dressed in their Sunday best. He hadn't seen them so clean and neat since before Ruth became sick, and he had to admit he liked the improvement. Maybe he should have bathed himself before dinner.

"It's us, Pa," Toby said.

"So it is. Both of you look mighty fine," Luke said as he sat down at the head of the table. "And what a lady you are, Miss Molly."

His daughter brightened at his compliment then said, "You really think so?"

"Yes, ma'am, I do," he told her. "I forgot what you looked like under all that grime. I think that I like you all dressed up."

"We don't have to stay like this, do we, Pa?" Toby asked.

"No, not all the time, but it's a nice change for dinner. Speaking of which," Luke glanced around the room. "Where is your nanny?"

"She said she was *very* tired. S--so she went to bed," Molly said, glancing furtively at her brother for help.

"Yeah, she looked *real* tired," Toby agreed, unsuccessfully hiding a smirk.

"Well, I guess she did have a long trip, and then bathing you two must have done her in."

Both children giggled as Maria entered carrying the platter of beef. Ada was right behind her with the bowls of potatoes and carrots slathered in butter.

"Let's go ahead and eat and let Miss Shannon rest," Luke instructed after Maria and Ada left them to dine. "Miss Shannon can join us tomorrow night." He served his children and himself then lifted his fork and knife when his gaze fell on the empty place setting to his left. Unbidden, a stab of regret moved through him. A Scottish brogue sounded in his ears, and he frowned upon realizing the meaning behind the sadness twisting in his gut. He realized that he'd been looking forward to seeing Shannon at dinner. And he was none too sure why.

Giving himself a mental shake, Luke cut into his meat. "What do you two think of your new nanny?"

"She's mean," Molly said.

Luke raised an eyebrow. "How so?"

"She locked us in the bathing room and told us we couldn't leave until we had a bath," Molly informed him. "I didn't like that." She set her fork down and crossed her arms over her chest defiantly.

"She locked you in there alone?" Heat crept up Luke's neck.

"Not exactly," Molly hedged. "She was in there with us."

"She scrubbed my face real good," Toby complained, his chin jutting stubbornly. "I bet my face was plum red when she'd finished!"

"I don't call that being mean," Luke told them. He reached for the gravy. "Sounds like she's doing her job to me. You both know you were filthy and needed a bath. Your mother would never have let you get so dirty."

"Well, Miss Shannon talks funny," Molly complained.

"Aye. That she does," Luke mocked.

"Oh no, Pa!" Toby rolled his eyes. "You're doin' it too."

Luke chuckled. "Just because someone doesn't talk the same as we do is no reason to not like them. Look at Maria. She doesn't speak like us, and we all like her." He smiled. "I have a feeling you could probably learn something from Miss Shannon."

Unexpectedly, he realized he was speaking up for the woman he didn't want around. He quickly changed the subject before he convinced himself to let her stay. "Now eat up. It's been a long day for all of us, and we need to get some shut-eye."

Once the children settled down, Luke enjoyed his meal. Tonight, he noticed that they talked more than usual at dinner. Each child told him their own version of the story about playing with the piglets, and how Miss Shannon had done this and that.

Luke tried to listen to them, but his mind kept drifting off to his new employee. He wanted to hear the sound of her voice, the lilting tones of her strange accent. He found her brogue very appealing, probably because it was so different from anything he'd heard around these parts. He really couldn't say he disliked the woman even if she had lied about her age. But she certainly didn't appear sturdy enough for this country. A flicker of apprehension coursed through him, thinking of his frail wife. Guilt tightened his throat as it always did when Ruth was foremost in his mind, and he sighed heavily. Would there ever come a day when he'd think of Ruth and not feel guilty?

Shoving her to the back of his mind, he turned his thoughts to Shannon. His nanny had thirty days to prove him right or wrong. Even if she was as stubborn as a mule, she'd see that he was right. In the meantime, he would have help with his children, something he desperately needed.

Miss Shannon had certainly made an improvement in their appearance, and she hadn't yet been here an entire day, Luke reluctantly admitted to himself. What would a full day with the feisty Scot be like?

"What you smilin' about, Pa?" Toby asked.

Caught in his daydream, Luke felt his face grow warm. "I was just thinking how nice both of you look tonight. I'm real proud that you're my children."

They both beamed at the compliment. Molly looked so much like her mother. Ruth would be pleased with the way they were growing up. And with that thought Luke's smile faded. "Time for bed," he announced abruptly.

Wasn't this what he'd employed a nanny for? Luke thought wryly as he followed his children to their rooms. Just like he thought, the woman wasn't strong enough to hold up out here; she hadn't even made it a full day before she'd taken to her bed. He supposed he could cut her some slack this time, since she'd made such a long journey. However, the minute she began to look sick, he was carting her back to town.

After Luke had gotten his children settled, he went to his wing of the house and straight to the bathing room attached to his bedroom. The tub had already been filled in anticipation of his needs, and he was glad that the staff was on the job.

"Damn, my shoulders are tight," he grumbled as he sank down into the steaming water. Hot water was exactly what he needed. Luke could remember how foolish he'd thought bathing rooms were when Ruth had suggested building them. Now he realized that he appreciated this small luxury more than he'd been willing to admit.

Following his bath, Luke dried off, wrapped the towel around his waist then strolled to the door connecting to his bedroom, thinking how quiet the house was tonight. It was quite a contrast to the normal atmosphere in his home. He wondered why the children had gone so willingly to bed this early. Normally, they fussed. Whatever the reason, he was glad for the quiet. It gave him a chance to think.

His thought also strayed to the situation in the Texas Territory. The political atmosphere in Texas had gone from peaceful and quiet to a general state of discontent. He had a feeling that there was going to be bloodshed before long. Santa Anna had made himself a dictator, and the Texas settlers were talking about freeing themselves from Mexico. Luke didn't want fighting near his home, but he would fight to protect it if he had to.

It had taken a lot of hard work to build the ranch up into what it had become, and he'd be damned if he'd let the Mexicans take it over. Maybe his brother would have some news on what was happening once he arrived.

Shrugging off his worries, Luke blew out the candle and opened the door to his bedroom, the pitch black of night surrounded him. Evidently, the maids had forgotten to leave a lamp on for him. Stripping off his towel, he pulled back the bedcovers. They didn't slip back as they normally did, but he didn't pay it much attention. The cool sheets felt good as he slipped beneath them, and . . . whoa, something heavy was on top of the covers. As he reached out to feel what the object was, his hand brushed across warm flesh. "What the hell?" he muttered, springing from the bed so fast it was a wonder he didn't break his fool neck. He stubbed his toe and saw stars as he fumbled to light a lamp.

He wasn't quite prepared for the sight that met his eyes.

Red hair fanned out across the white covers, Miss McKinley was lying across his bed sound asleep. What the blazes was the woman doing here in his bed? The sight of her scantily clad body made his blood run hot. She was in her drawers for Christ's sake.

Slowly, Shannon's eyes flickered opened. She rubbed them, confused. Then she saw Luke standing before her, naked as the day he was born. She bolted straight up in bed and screamed.

Luke leaped across the bed and clamped a hand over her mouth. "For Christ's sake, woman, quit that screeching. You'll wake the entire house!"

Wild-eyed, she looked at him over his hand.

"If you promise not to scream, I'll remove my hand. I'm not going to attack you, so you can get that fool notion out of your head." When she nodded he uncovered her mouth and slid back off the bed.

"Fool notion, indeed!" she said, her voice indignant, though she wasn't looking at him. "What are ye doin' in my room?"

"Your room? What the Sam Hill are you doing in *my* room?" Luke barked back.

Shannon finally looked at him, her eyes widened, before she put her hands to her flaming cheeks and said in a lower voice, "I'm not that kind o' woman, I'll huv ye know. Put yer clothes back on, mon," she added primly as she averted her eyes.

Luke glanced down and only then did he remember that he wasn't wearing a stitch of clothes. "Shit!" He snatched up the towel from the floor and wrapped it around himself. "So what are you doing in *my* room?"

Shannon's head was reeling. The man was stark naked, and had the bloody nerve to yell at her. She peeked between her fingers to find that he had, at least, covered himself. Slowly, she let her hands down, but in doing so loosened the shoulder strap of her chemise, exposing a breast. She squealed, yanked the strap back up, and grabbed the afghan that had fallen off her, then covered herself.

"'Twas my understanding that this was my room," she said, her brow rising as she tried to look haughty.

Luke couldn't keep his gaze from where her breast had been showing. Shaking his head to rid himself of unwanted thoughts, he said, "I don't know where you got such a fool notion like that. Your room is in the other wing of the house with the children. That's where the nannies sleep." Luke came around to her side of the bed and stopped in front of her.

In spite of his anger and surprise, his body was acting quite the opposite. There was something damn strange about this woman. Why was he so attracted to her?

Well, hell. It was obvious.

With her hair hanging loose around her shoulders, Shannon appeared much younger than she had this afternoon. And quite beautiful in a way he'd not noticed earlier. "Just how young are you?"

"'Tisn't a question one usually asks a woman. And if asked at all 'tis how *old* are ye, not how young," she retorted primly.

Luke raised a brow. "You did everything but answer my question. How old are you?"

"I'm one and twenty."

At least she was a little older than he'd first thought. However she didn't look it. "I should have left you in town."

"Well, ye dinna, so yer stuck with me until the next stage comes," she retorted in that sassy style he was coming to love -- and hate. Luke wondered if the woman knew how lovely she really was.

After a moment, Shannon calmed down. "Apparently, I made a mistake tonight by thinkin' this was my room." She wasn't going to let him know that his little imps had tricked her. "If ye like, I'll get dressed, and ye can show me tae where I do belong."

Luke wasn't quite sure what had gotten into him, but he reached out and brushed the hair from her shoulder before he could stop himself. She didn't jump away from his touch, but he couldn't miss her quick intake of breath. She was much too temping as she was now. For a moment, their eyes met, and he saw Ruth, and he felt as if he'd been doused with ice water.

Immediately, he stepped back, his emotions feeling as if they were tumbling over a waterfall and he had no control of them. And he liked being in control. "Look, you go ahead and sleep in here tonight, and I'll sleep in your room."

"Are ye sure?"

"Yeah, it will be easier. In the morning, we'll get your sleeping arrangements straightened out."

"Thanks. I was sleepin' verra well until ye woke me."

"Apparently," Luke said matter-of-factly, but he couldn't help his slight smile. He headed for the bathing room, stopping to light a candle so he didn't break his neck on the way to the other wing, but before leaving, he turned and said,

"Enjoy my bed tonight. Tomorrow you'll sleep in your own."

After he'd left, Shannon pulled the patch-worked quilt back and slipped between the sheets. So this was Luke's room, she thought as she stretched out amongst the pillows. No wonder it had seemed so grand. She glanced around before she blew out the lamp. The dark furniture was much like its master ... hard ... unmoving.

She could get used to this room. A slow smile touched her lips. She had to admit that Luke was one fine mon. Perhaps, he was a wee bit temperamental, but, she'd wager, with a bit of work, maybe she could loosen him up.

A cowboy of her own? And now she had one within her grasp, Shannon smiled again. He just didn't know it yet. Of course, she'd have to make sure she could get along with his children. She had already seen they were quite a handful.

The little devils had purposely steered her into the wrong room. They might not have thought far enough ahead to think that their father could have taken advantage of her, but they had known that there would be fireworks. Shannon's face still felt hot at the thought of the magnificent naked man. Of course, she'd only caught the briefest glimpse . . . but, oh Lord, the mon was muscular in all the right places.

Hadn't she always said she wanted a husband and children? Now she had the opportunity . . . Well, sort of . . . the children's behavior was questionable, and their father didn't appear to want to marry anyone, much less her.

Then again, men didn't usually know what they wanted when it came to home and family. Shannon smiled. Unless a woman pointed it out.

She rolled over in bed. She'd felt her body react when Luke was near her and had to admit she wouldn't mind having strong arms around her. What would it be like to be kissed by Luke? Was he as wild as the west? With such delicious thoughts tumbling through her mind, she closed her eyes and drifted into the land of dreams where she was in control of everything.

THE NEXT MORNING it took several minutes before Shannon remembered where she was, but as soon as she did, she slid out of bed. It was still early, and she wanted a bath before breakfast.

She was pondering just how she was going to accomplish the task when someone knocked on the door. Surely it wasn't Luke coming to claim his room already.

Since she didn't even have her robe to dress in, she wrapped herself in the quilt and went to the door. Opening it a crack, she saw a young woman dressed similar to Maria. The woman was more like a girl with long black hair, dressed in a sky blue skirt. She had something draped over her arm.

"Good morning, Señorita Shannon. Señor Luke said maybe you like a bath and clean clothes."

"Aye, 'twould be wonderful," Shannon answered gratefully. "Is that my gown that ye huv there?"

"*Sí,*" she said with a nod.

Shannon opened the door. "Come in."

The pert girl, who looked about the same age as herself and with dark skin, swept in and placed the gown on the bed. "The trunks, they already are in your room," she said, "but since you're not there, Señor had me choose a gown for you. I hope this one is all right."

The girl had picked out a yellow day dress – one of

Shannon's favorites. "Aye, 'tis fine. But I'll huv tae put on my dress from yesterday tae go tae the bathing room in the other part of the house."

"Oh, no," the girl said, crossing to the door that Luke had opened last night. She opened the door and swept her hand inward. "There is a bathing room," she pointed, "in here and the tub has already been filled, so you can bathe and dress in private."

Shannon wondered what the girl must think of her being in Luke's room, dressed in only her chemise. She couldn't imagine the maid having ever encountered a woman other than Ruth in Luke's room before. But then maybe she had. Shannon had to admit she didn't know the man that well

Shannon followed the girl into the next room, surprised to find everything was ready for her. This room was a little different from the one she'd seen yesterday. There was only one tub, but she could tell that a woman had decorated the room because of the many beautiful landscape paintings hanging on the walls. However, it wasn't the beauty that caught her eye and kept it, but a pair of men's boots.

They stood by the tub and seeing them immediately produced an image of the naked cowboy who had stood by the bed last night and made her body tingle.

"'Tis a bit hot this mornin'," Shannon said, fanning herself, hoping that the girl hadn't noticed how red her face had become.

The young woman hurried over and picked up the boots. "Señor Luke told me to get these for him." This time the girl blushed.

Shannon knew exactly what the girl must be thinking. "What is yer name?" she asked to distract herself from the delicious images forming in her mind.

"Carmen."

"Well, Carmen, I want tae thank ye for coming tae my rescue. It seems I was a bit confused aboot which room was mine."

"Oh, there is no need to explain, señorita," Carmen rushed to assure her. "Do you need any help dressing? I will come back."

"Nay. The gown ye chose fastens in the front, so I'll be fine. Besides, I work here the same as ye."

The girl's eyes widened with surprise, but she didn't say anything. She nodded, then disappeared back into the bedroom, closing the door behind her.

Shannon stepped into the high tub and slid down into the glorious hot water. She'd never felt so wonderful in all her life. All the stress from the last several days seeped out of her body as she soaked.

Shannon could see that she took her comfortable life back in England very much for granted. She'd grown up with servants to do everything for her, even when she lived in her father's home, so she wasn't certain she knew how to be a servant. But she was going to try. She knew Brooke and Jocelyn had thought her crazy for accepting this position, and maybe she was. She had inherited enough money from her Uncle Jackson to support herself for a little while. She guessed she could go back to New Orleans where Brooke lived if things didn't work out here, but that wasn't what Shannon really wanted. She wanted to make it on her own, too, believing in hard work. And most of all Shannon wanted her own family.

She just had to find love and where she belonged. She was attracted to Luke Griffin, she admitted. And she had a definite feeling he was attracted to her. Whether he wanted to be or not.

Shannon hoped that the entire household didn't think she'd shared a bed with Luke. Saints above, she'd just arrived. They'd think she was a loose woman, a hussy. She didn't want that. Then again, maybe they also knew that he'd slept in the bed where she should have been.

Those children! From now on, she'd know better than to trust them.

After her bath, she pulled her hair up with two combs and let it fall loose and free over her shoulders. She was tired of the small, tight ringlets that were all the rage. Besides which, she had no one to style her hair so loose was easier. Taking the lemon-yellow dress off the bed, she wondered what the day would bring. She stepped into her chemise and then the day dress. There was no need for petticoats in Texas. This dress had a high bodice, draped with folds, which would give her easier movement with the children, something she was sure she'd need.

Shannon had noticed that her gowns were much fancier than the clothing she'd seen women in Texas wearing so far. She'd thought to bring her plainest outfits with her, yet even those were too fancy. Of course, she did have a few blouses and skirts that would probably be more suitable. Tomorrow she'd make sure they were unpacked and shaken out.

Since she wasn't certain of the time, she decided to check the dining room before going to fetch the children. She hurried down the quiet halls, wondering what the children would think up to annoy her today or what tricks they might have up their sleeves.

She stopped short just inside the door. What she didn't expect was to find everyone already seated and eating.

"Good morning," Luke said when she peeked into the room. He pointed to the chair next to him, the one across from the children. "This is your place."

"Och, I'm late. I was a wee bit disoriented after last night," she said as she swept into the room. "I'm feeling much better this morning." She stopped behind her chair and waited for Luke to pull out the chair for her. However he was eating and not paying her any attention ... then she remembered her station and seated herself. She settled herself across from the children, who were innocently smiling at her as if they'd done nothing wrong.

"Good morning," Shannon said to the children with a bright cheerful smile.

"Mornin,'" they both murmured, and then instantly found their plates very interesting.

Luke handed her a platter of ham. "Just how did you end up in my room? Surely Maria didn't take you to it."

Shannon placed a slice of ham on her plate, before she glanced up at the children, who continued looking down at their plates. For a moment, she chose not to answer the question and calmly buttered her toast. Let the wee ones worry just a mite. 'Twould serve them right. She wondered how long they could hold their breath.

"Perhaps the question was too hard," Luke commented.

Shannon glanced at Luke. "Nay, Maria dinna show me tae my room. I assumed the children were in one wing and the adults in another. Probably comes from bein' so tired."

Turning back to the children who were now staring at her, mouths gaping, she wanted to reach across the table and push their mouths shut, but instead she let them stew.

"Is there anything ye'd like the children tae do today?" Shannon asked Luke.

"No. I'll leave that up to you."

"I thought I'd huv them do their school work in the mornings. And –"

"Ah, Pa. We don't want to do no school work," Toby protested.

Shannon glanced at the boy. "Do ye want tae be ignorant the rest o' yer life?"

"What's ignorant?" Toby asked.

"Ye would know if ye'd been taught properly," Shannon retorted, enjoying the feeling of satisfaction.

"I agree. They do need to do their lessons," Luke said. He shoved back from the table. "I'll leave the children to you. However, I'll be working out on the north range today. You can send a rider out if you need me." He looked at his children pointedly as he continued, "And you really shouldn't need me."

Shannon nodded. So he still didn't think she could do the job. She'd have to show him. "We'll be fine. Won't we children?"

All she saw were two frowning children who reluctantly nodded their heads. Shannon wondered what manner of devious tricks they had planned for her today. She supposed she'd soon find out.

At least, today she'd be prepared.

*a*n hour later, once the children discovered Shannon was serious about their schoolwork, they stopped pouting. However, their pouting wasn't the problem. She discovered that Molly recognized a scant few words, and Toby couldn't read at all. Granted, he was young, but Shannon was determined these children would learn something before she left.

She hadn't had a chance to go to her room yet -- and she certainly wasn't going to ask the children for directions again -- so she could get a few school books. However, Shannon remembered an old reader, which her mother had used to teach her to read, and it just happened to be in her reticule. She dug down into her bag and brought out the well-worn and well-loved book.

The children took their places at the small desks she assumed Luke had built. A larger wooden table for the teacher stood in front of the room. It was a quaint schoolroom complete with chalkboards and slates, proving that their parents had cared about their education. Shannon wondered if their mother had taught them the little they knew before she died.

"I want ye both tae come up here and stand on each side of me. I'm going tae teach ye how tae read."

After they had taken their places, she cleared her throat and began reading. Since the story was about Roman soldiers, it kept the children's interest as she taught them to sound out each word. Of course, Molly, being older, caught on a little faster, but Toby was a fighter determined not to be left behind. He wanted to do everything his sister did. Only he wanted to do it sooner, faster and better. Shannon could see some of his father's mannerisms in the child, especially his stubbornness.

It was nearing the noon hour when she said, "Next, we'll do arithmetic so ye can go back tae yer desk."

"We're tired," Molly complained.

"And hungry," Toby added.

"I'm a wee bit hungry myself," Shannon admitted. "We'll get something tae eat before we huv our next lesson."

Toby rolled his eyes. "Ah, do we have to have more lessons?"

"Learning can be fun," Shannon insisted. "But lessons dinna all huv tae come from books. We'll go outside fer our next lesson. 'Tis a game."

"Are you funning us?" asked Toby as he drew his brows together suspiciously.

"Nay. Ye'll see."

Molly stood and asked, a look of doubt in her eyes, "What kind of a game?"

"I'll tell ye after our meal."

They marched toward the kitchen, Shannon in the rear, making sure neither of her students bolted at the first chance they got. Once in the kitchen, they headed toward the large, trestle table. The kids ran to take their places. It was so much more comfortable here, Shannon thought as she relaxed. The kitchen was warm and inviting. The cooks had raised the windows to alleviate some of the heat coming from the wood stove.

Fond childhood memories came to her as she took her place at the table. When she was a child, she'd love to sneak off to the kitchen to eat with the servants because they were always so kind and welcoming. She felt completely at home in the kitchen, and she'd bet the Griffin children did too.

The kitchen staff was busy bustling about as usual, and the aroma of what was probably to be the evening meal was already cooking. It smelled wonderful.

"I was wondering when you wanted to eat," Maria said as she brought over plates of white flat things and beans and some kind of chopped meat. She handed everyone a plate and silverware.

"What is this?" Shannon asked.

"You've had this, *sí*?"

"Nay," Shannon replied.

Maria smiled. "It's tortillas and refried beans. You fill the tortilla with beans and meat and roll it up like the *niños*, *sí*."

Shannon followed the instructions and then took a bite. She wiped her mouth. It was a bit different from the fare she'd been accustomed to, but after the first bite, she decided it most certainly was tasty. "This is wonderful. I guess I've learned something new today."

"*Sí*, very good. And the *niños*, what have you been doing?"

"We've been learnin'," Toby offered, puffing his small chest out proudly.

"I believe Señorita Shannon will be able to teach you

much things," Maria said as she poured the milk into glasses.

Shannon noticed both children frowned in response to Maria's statement. What a stubborn lot they were. However, Shannon didn't let on that she'd noticed their reactions.

After she finished eating, Maria took her aside and said, "I understand you went to the wrong room last night, señorita."

"Aye." Shannon said, feeling the heat of embarrassment stain her cheeks. She let out a barely noticeable sigh, "'Twas a bit of a misunderstanding, I'm afraid."

"*Sí*. Those *niños* can be a handful, can they not? Come with me, señorita. While they finish eating, I take you to your proper room," Maria said, spearing the children with a knowing glance.

Toby and Molly didn't flinch at all. They wore that same innocent look perfected from years of practice, Shannon supposed.

"I'll be back in a moment. I expect tae find ye here, ready tae learn when I return," she told them firmly.

Maria led Shannon to the children's wing. "I'm so sorry for the mistake. You would do best to remember you cannot trust the *niños*. They want always to play games, and the nanny is their favorite target."

"Aye, so I found out."

Maria pushed open a door at the end of the hall, and Shannon looked inside. What she found was a room a little bit bigger than the children's, decorated in brown and white.

"'Tis a bit drab," Shannon said, "But 'twill be fine." She spotted her luggage lined up neatly against the wall. "I see my things huv been delivered. Perhaps, tonight I'll huv time tae put my clothing away." She managed a wry smile. "At least there wull be no mistakes made tonight."

"*Sí*, Señorita," Maria agreed.

Shannon thanked Maria, then said, "I had better go back tae the children before they find somethin' else tae get into."

"*Sí*, let's see if they are still there."

"Perhaps, they'll wait since I promised tae show them something new." Shannon smiled, then added, "Sometimes bribery works best."

SHANNON FOUND the children sitting at the table, waiting patiently, something they had surely never done before, she wagered. It was a small victory, but one she would gladly take.

"Are ye ready tae go outside fer yer next lesson?" She clapped her hands together in what she hoped was an authoritative manner. Then she remembered she shouldn't have asked a question but told them they were going outside, since she was the one in charge.

Toby and Molly nodded eagerly. It was the first time Shannon had seen them excited about anything, and it was a nice change.

Once outside, she led them around to the side of the house where she had seen a smooth patch of dirt. "Now ye need tae find a throwin' stone, not tae big. About this size," she said, holding her finger and thumb in a small circle that approximated the right size. "And, Toby, can ye find me a sturdy stick?"

He nodded, his chest puffing up with importance. He began scouting around. In the meantime, Shannon found a flat, smooth rock that would work beautifully.

Molly had already found her stone and stood quietly watching, her expression interested, but aloof.

In a few minutes, Toby had returned with a three foot sick. "Whatcha need this for?" He brandished it, swatting it through the air as if he were dueling.

"Ye'll see." No sense telling them what was going on too soon. She wanted to keep their interest.

Toby held up his rock, a small white stone about the size of a flattened marble. "Is this one big enough, Miss Shannon?"

"'Tis perfect. We're goin' tae play a game called hopscotch."

"What's that?" they both asked at the same time.

"I'm glad ye asked," Shannon said, marveling that they weren't familiar with the simple game. "Remember when we read about the soldiers earlier?"

They nodded.

"Hopscotch is a game that began in the early Roman Empire.

"The original hopscotch courts were over one hundred feet long and used tae train the soldiers. Ours wull not be that big, since we're not trainin' fer battle," she said with a smile. "Back then, the Roman foot-soldiers ran the court, what they called a course, in full armor and field packs tae improve their footwork. Their children became fascinated with the game and drew their own smaller courts tae imitate the solders, but they added a scorin' system. Do ye understand?"

They nodded with confused expressions. "But how do you play?" Molly asked.

"First, let me draw the court." Shannon watched them out of the corner of her eye as she slowly and deliberately took the stick from Toby and drew the blocks in the dirt. There were three single squares, a doubled square followed by another single square, another double square and one final single square. When she'd finished drawing, she returned to the end with the three single squares. "I'll go first, since ye dinna know how tae play."

"Hey! That's not fair," Toby protested. "You're the teacher."

"Aye." Shannon smiled. "And as such I'm goin' tae teach ye how tae play."

Shannon wanted to laugh. She knew she had the children's full attention, and she liked it. They stared curiously at the court she'd drawn out. She waited, letting their curiosity build.

"All right," Shannon said. "Place yer marker in the first square next tae mine," she instructed as she tossed her stone in the first block. "Remember which one is yours. Rule number one: Ye canna step in a square with a stone in it. And when ye toss yer marker, it canna land on the line, nor canna it bounce out either. If it does, ye'll forfeit yer turn."

"What does f--forfeit mean?" Toby asked.

"It means ye lose yer turn."

They both nodded that they understood. Then each one stepped to the line and dropped their stone in the first block.

"Now I'm going tae begin," Shannon said. "I must hop on one foot in the single squares. In the double squares, ye can straddle them, with the left foot landing in the left square and the right foot in the right square. But, remember, I canna step in a square that has a stone in it."

Suddenly, the hair on the back of Shannon's neck prickled. A feeling of being watched settled over her. She jerked her head to the right and stared at a clump of trees on a hill in the distance. Why did she feel like someone was watching them? She didn't see anything.

"What's wrong?" Toby asked.

"I thought I'd seen something in the trees but it must huv been my imagination."

She hiked her skirts up and began to hop as the children watched her. Toby giggled at the ridiculous sight. This had seemed so much easier when she was younger, Shannon thought as she wobbled, struggling to keep her balance. She breathed a relieved sigh when she reached the end, paused for a moment in the top square, and then turned around. On the way back, she stooped down, balancing on one foot, to pick up her stone, and then hopped out. "Now I get tae go again."

"That's not fair." Toby protested. "I want a turn."

"Aye, but 'tis. If I lose my balance or step on a line or miss the block then 'tis yer turn. I'll warn ye, I used tae be pretty good at this game when I was small," she boasted.

She tossed the stone and once again hitched up her skirts, taking a running leap to jump over the first two blocks and make it safely to the third. She wobbled, flailing her arms, as she tried to regain her balance. She made it and began to hop again.

After she picked up her stone and got ready to make her third throw, she noticed the two very long faces of her students. So she deliberately tossed the stone astray. It landed on the line, and she had to forfeit her turn.

"Goodie. It's my turn," Toby announced.

"No, it isn't! It's mine," Molly argued.

"Girls first." Both children whipped around to face Shannon.

"Molly can go first this time, and the next game Toby will be first," Shannon told them firmly, her tone brooking no argument. Surprisingly, neither protested the decision. Instead, they began to play.

They both were quite good, and before long, they were

on their third game of hopscotch. Molly had won the first game and Toby the second. It was a draw, and it was time for a tiebreaker. This time, Shannon would show no mercy. After all, she had to show them who was best.

As Luke rode toward the ranch, he had to admit he was glad to be heading home because he'd had to force himself to concentrate on the fence job all morning. He kept wondering how the children were doing. That's why he jumped on the chance to go and fetch dinner for the crew.

He spotted the children and Shannon doing something beside the house. He turned his horse so that he rode up behind the barn. This would give him a chance to observe without being noticed.

Luke stood at the corner of the barn watching his children and his nanny hopping around like a bunch of rabbits.

What in the world were they doing? Hopping?

He watched a while longer, amazed that they were so engaged in whatever they were doing instead of fighting. The best he could tell, they seemed to be playing a game, but what they were playing puzzled him. To his surprise, the children were laughing and enjoying themselves. How long had it been since they were so carefree? Usually they were in trouble. Sometimes Luke felt all he did was yell at them.

And the nanny was still here. It was downright amazing.

He figured she'd be long gone by the time he came back to the house.

Then to Luke's amazement, Shannon hiked up her skirts exposing delicate ankles . . . a very nice sight indeed. She began hopping on one foot just as the children had. Puzzled, he decided to watch for a few minutes more unobserved, and see how they were getting along.

"I thought you were good at this game, Miss Shannon," Molly teased.

"I used tae be," Shannon retorted as she struggled to keep her balance. "But somehow it seems different than what I remember. 'Tis what happens when ye get older."

"How has it gotten different?" Toby asked, then yelled, "Watch out! You almost stepped on the line."

"I missed it, though." Shannon paused a moment, frowning down at him. "Wull, fer one thing, I've gotten taller and my feet are much bigger, sae I'm at a disadvantage," she said, making her excuses as she made it to the top of the squares. Then she turned. "All I huv tae do is make it back, and I'll win."

She started hopping again. Luke could tell that Shannon was tired by the way her foot kept easing lower. That she was playing with his children, at all, surprised him. The other nannies hadn't bothered. Shannon only had a few more squares to go when she lost her balance and fell backwards to the ground, landing on her bottom and sending puffs of dust in the air.

The children giggled. Then Molly shouted gleefully, "I win! I win! Let's play again."

Sensing that Miss Shannon needed to rest, Luke strolled around the corner toward them. "Now, now. It isn't nice to laugh when someone falls," he told the children as he bent down, offering Shannon his hand. She took it gratefully, and he hauled her to her feet.

"But she's laughing," Toby said.

And sure enough, once she had swept that glorious red hair from her face, he could see she was laughing, too. It was a refreshing sound, and not often heard around his home.

Life and laughter seemed to sparkle in her eyes and radiated from somewhere deep inside Shannon. No matter how prim and proper she tried to be, that sparkle always broke though. The sparkle that made her different.

Dang, she was beautiful. He'd have to be dead not to notice the rose color in her cheeks and the brightness of her eyes. And her mouth was much too inviting. It made him think of things he hadn't thought about in quite a long time.

Things he had no right to think about.

"'Tis all right for them tae laugh," Shannon said in the children's defense. She brushed off her skirts. "We were playing a game, and I simply lost my balance," she explained in a voice that was becoming all too familiar to him. A problem, he realized.

Toby was tossing his rock in the air and catching it when he said, "You should see the new game we just learned."

"A game?" Luke turned to Shannon. "I thought you were going to teach them from books," he said, his tone accusing.

"We're learning, Pa," Molly informed him, then pointed to the drawing in the dirt. "This is what Roman soldiers used to do."

"See." Toby tossed his stone in the first square. "You do it like this."

Luke patiently watched his son hop flawlessly through the course. When Toby had finished, he handed his father a stone. "You try, Pa. It's lots of fun."

"From the laughter I just heard, I can see it was. But I'll have to take your word for it now because I need to ride back out. I just came to fetch some grub," Luke said. He reached for Shannon's elbow, then addressed the children. "Go ahead and finish your game. I'm going to borrow Miss Shannon for a moment."

As they walked away from the children, Shannon challenged, "Are ye afraid tae play a game?"

"I'm too old for such nonsense," Luke stated firmly. "Besides, I have too much work to do."

She stopped and looked at him. "I thought that is why ye huv ranch hands." She saw that her remark irritated him but then again, what didn't? "Besides, yer not that old. Ye know, sometimes I think ye've forgotten how tae smile."

Luke caught her arm so suddenly that it made her want to jump back. He led her farther away from the children before he turned on her. "Let me tell you something, Miss McKinley. You've only been here a day and a half, so I'll let your comment slide as ignorance."

Shannon drew back to give him a piece of her mind, but he anticipated her move and placed his finger across her lips. One touch sent cold shivers skittering down her spine in spite of her anger.

"Let me finish. You're not in your fancy ballrooms anymore. You're in a rough country that was wild only a few years ago. There isn't a lot to smile about out here . . . just damned hard work. And when there isn't work, there are skirmishes with the Mexicans who want to take back their land. If you get sick, the nearest doctor is in Cottonwood, and you have to be real lucky not to die before he drives out here. So I'm sorry that we can't be more entertaining, Miss McKinley." Luke didn't add that there used to be laugher in his house when his wife was alive. Since her death he'd been even more determined to make a success of this ranch.

Shannon folded her arms across her chest as she waited for Luke to finish his rant. She hadn't taken her eyes off his face and realized that if he hadn't been so blistering mad, she was close enough to kiss him. That thought almost made her smile. A kiss would certainly shut him up, and quickly, too. Instead she said, "Are ye finished?"

"Yep."

"I see ye must huv had a bad mornin' and, perhaps, yer hearin' isn't as good as it should be. I was not complainin', mon. I merely pointed out that ye could smile for yer children once in awhile. Dinna ye see how their faces light up when ye come around? How proud they were tae show ye what they'd learned today? I bet ye smiled a lot before their mother died."

"That's none of your business."

"Aye, but the children are. Dinna punish them fer their mother's death."

Luke stepped closer to her, but Shannon stood her ground. "If you were a man, I'd punch you."

She gave him a slow smile. "Being a lady does huv its advantages," she said sweetly. With that remark Luke felt all his bluster drift away, and he took a step back and rubbed the back of his neck.

"I believe ye wanted tae talk tae me," she pointed out.

"To tell you the truth, I don't remember what I wanted you for," he said vaguely, his thoughts obviously somewhere else. "Frankly, I'm surprised you're still here."

"And exactly where would I be goin'?" she asked though she didn't wait for his answer. "After all, I huv a job tae do."

As Luke watched the sassy Scot walk away from him, his gaze drifted down to hips that swayed seductively beneath the material of her skirt. "Only thirty days," he mumbled.

"Make that twenty-eight days," he corrected himself. He just hoped he could survive until the stage came. Then he'd put her on it and send her back to where she came from, but with that thought came a twinge of sadness over not seeing her again. He shook his head . . . must be the sun. He needed to keep his priorities straight.

A CLUMP of cottonwoods surrounded by sagebrush made a perfect cover for someone to hide. It had taken Alasdair and Callum a while to find the ranch. Why the lass would come way out here puzzled them both.

Alasdair looked through his spyglass. "I can see the lass. Looks like she is playing with the children."

"Do ye see any way tae get at her?" Callum asked.

"Nay. I saw the mon ride out this mornin' but now he's back. I think it best tae watch fer a few days and see what kind of routine they huv around here."

"Perhaps we can catch her if she goes tae the barn," Callum said as he tugged on his shirt. "This God awful heat should tell the lass that she no belongs in this country. She needs tae go home. Maybe she wull see that herself. 'Twould make our lives easier."

"I dinna think so, Callum."

"Why do ye say that, Alasdair?"

"'Cause the lass looks happy. When is the last time ye've seen her happy?"

"Not since her mother died."

"Once she's married, she wull be happy enough. Not much we can do now." Callum reached in his bag and pulled out some bread and cheese.

Alasdair closed his spyglass. "One of us could hire on as a ranch hand sae we could get closer."

Callum laughed, putting his hand over his mouth to keep quiet, then he handed Alasdair a slice of cheese. "Ye dinna think they'd recognize our accents? 'Sides the lass would run as soon as she spotted us."

Alasdair laughed too. "I'd no thought aboot how strange they sound around here. Sounds more like they are gruntin' all the time."

7

*H*ad it been almost a month?

The days had whirled by for Shannon, but now she had to wonder if Luke would send her away as he'd initially threatened. There were times when she'd catch him staring at her, apparently for no reason at all. She'd thought by now she would have known him a little better, yet she was unable to tell what was on his mind. Did he think she was doing a good job? Or, did he still wish he'd left her in Cottonwood? Shannon wished she knew. The one thing she did know . . . Luke was a good person.

Shannon had settled into the household despite the lizards and frogs put in her room two weeks ago. The children soon found out she didn't scare easily. She smiled, remembering when she returned the favor by leaving two lizards in the children's room. She could still hear them screaming. Shannon thought that was a good lesson they wouldn't soon forget.

Thankfully, Molly and Toby hadn't tried any tricks in the last couple of days, but she wasn't sure they had completely reformed. She wasn't going to let her guard down so soon.

At least, they were not rejecting her at every turn. Now it was more like a truce. But, of course, those two could have a relapse at any time.

Shannon had to admit that she was proud of the way the children were learning to read. Molly, being the oldest, could read much better than Toby, but Toby was determined to catch up with his sister, so he kept asking for things to read. He was anxious to learn every subject, and as he put it . . . "I want to be just like Pa."

Shannon wanted to purchase a few books for the children. The books in Luke's bookcases were too advanced for them to read. Of course, she realized books might be something hard to come by out here in the middle of nowhere. Perhaps, she could write, her sister, Jocelyn, and have her send a few children's books to the ranch. Shannon needed to write her sisters anyway to let her know that she had arrived safely. She could also tell them about her cowboy. The problem was she didn't know enough about Luke to tell anyone anything.

Shannon sighed. She knew she'd found the man she wanted. The problem was figuring out how she could become a part of his life when he didn't seem to want her. He was as much a mystery today as the day she arrived. The only thing she could say about him in certainty was that he was methodical, and he didn't like surprises. How could she get Luke to open up and talk to her?

It was almost dinnertime, a time which Shannon looked forward to because Luke always ate with them. Then she could talk to him about his day or simply watch him without his noticing, and he seemed to enjoy dinner as much as she did. She had to admit that with each day she was more and more taken with the man. Yet, there was still so much she wanted to know about him. He guarded his thoughts and emotions so well she wasn't sure she'd ever break down the barrier he'd erected.

Unfortunately, Luke seemed totally unaffected by her presence. It was as if he didn't see her. He reminded her of someone just going through the motions of living.

ONE NIGHT BEFORE DINNER, Shannon heard Toby yell. "He's here! He's here!"

She couldn't imagine who the "he" was, but her curiosity made her hurry from her room. She didn't recognize the voice as she neared the main room. She heard the children's laughter mingled with a stranger's voice and realized that the children really liked him. She peered around the corner to see him.

"Do me. Do me!" Toby squealed with his arms held straight up in the air.

She watched the tall dark-haired stranger toss each child up in the air, his muscular arms catching them with ease. The room was filled with giggles.

The man's hair was darker than Luke's, and the stranger might be a little taller. But from what she could see, he was a strapping man and someone the children definitely were glad to see.

"I see we huv company," Shannon finally said, making her presence known.

"No, we don't." Toby giggled. "This is Uncle Travis. He ain't company."

"He *isn't* company," Shannon automatically corrected.

The cowboy turned toward her, his eyes alight with devilment as he said, "And who, may I ask, is this?" He directed his question to the children. "Your Pa didn't say anything about getting himself married."

"She's our nanny," Molly told him. "We've only had her a few weeks."

"A few weeks," Travis said, rubbing the top of Toby's head. "From what I understand, that's a record for you two."

"Oh, Uncle Travis," Molly said.

Shannon extended her hand. "Hello, my name is Shannon McKinley."

"You're a brave one." Travis took her hand and held it longer than was proper. He reminded her of some of the rakes she'd met in England. He had the same twinkle in his eye and devilish grin.

"So I've been told."

"I can't tell you how happy I am to meet you," he said. "The children have needed somebody for a long time, and I can see my brother made a good choice for a change." Travis gave her a big smile. "I think I'm going to like you."

Luke chose that exact moment to join them. "Unhand Miss McKinley."

"You're no fun, brother," Travis said, releasing Shannon and turning toward Luke. Travis slapped Luke on the back. "Just as ornery as ever, I see."

"Some of us don't have a carefree life like you do," Luke grumbled, then said, "You're early. Didn't expect you until tomorrow. But, you're just in time for dinner. Let's go to the dining room." Luke motioned in that direction.

"Sounds good. I need some of Maria's good cooking. Speaking of which," Travis offered his arm to Shannon, "May I escort you to dinner?"

Shannon laughed, then placed her hand on his arm. She found Travis's devilish personality refreshing. This house needed some laughter.

"Why does Uncle Travis have to show Miss Shannon where to eat?" Toby asked his sister. "She already knows where the dining room is."

Shannon heard Luke grumble. "Your uncle is just being a jackass."

"That's not nice, Pa," Molly informed her father.

Shannon thought Luke sounded jealous, however, she doubted that was the case, even if she did like the idea.

She sat in her normal place, and Travis took the chair to her right, with Luke at his usual seat at the head of the table. The servants brought in two roasted chickens, rice and vegetables and placed the hot dishes on the table.

After filling their plates, Luke asked Travis, "So what have you been up to?"

"Volunteered to help out the Texas army," Travis said.

Luke lowered his fork. "Texas has an army?"

"Nearly three hundred men. After a few Texans drove off the Mexican troops at Gonzales, Sam Houston decided to form an army. We elected Austin commander. I'll fill you in later. Right now, I want to know more about your nanny." Travis turned to Shannon. "Where are you from, Miss McKinley? That's not a Texas accent I'm hearing."

Shannon laughed. "Indeed, it isn't. I'm from Scotland, and please call me Shannon. As yer bother informed me, there is no need fer formality in Texas."

It was Travis's turn to laugh. "Luke told you correctly, but if you don't mind me asking, why are you so far away from home?"

Luke's fork hit the plate. "For Christ's sake, Travis, don't be so nosy."

"Just curious," he shot back. "I'm sure you've not bothered to ask her anything, but you have to admit it isn't every day we see a foreigner." Travis' gaze once again shifted to Shannon with a bemused smile on his lips.

"What's a foreigner?" Toby asked.

"Travis means somebody not from 'round here," Luke answered.

"Yer country has always fascinated me," Shannon admitted. "When my uncle died, his solicitor was able tae find a job fer me," she paused, "and since I'm fond of children, I thought 'twould be a good way tae do both of the things I wanted tae do." She took a sip of tea, then asked. "And what line of work are ye in?"

"I could listen to you talk all day." Travis grinned, then answered. "I travel around a lot."

"He's a drifter," Luke snapped.

"I am not."

Toby frowned. "What's a drifter?"

Travis glanced at his nephew. "A drifter is someone who doesn't know where he's going. However, I always know where I'm going, so I'm not a drifter."

Shannon had finished the apple pie that had been served for dessert. It had been a fine meal and Travis had proved a welcome addition at the table. He could liven up a meal. She wondered at the difference in the two men.

"Perhaps, I should put the children tae bed," Shannon said as she stood. "That way ye can have a private conversation." She didn't bother to add and finish your arguing.

"But we want to talk to Uncle Travis," Molly protested.

Travis stood too. "I'm going to stay a couple of days, so we'll have plenty of time to talk, Molly."

"Then we shall see ye tomorrow," Shannon said. "Children..." She held out her hand for them.

Molly and Toby kissed their father and Travis good night, then met Shannon at the door.

She turned and said, "Good night, Luke. Travis."

"Miss Shannon," Luke and Travis both said with a slight nod.

Luke's frown told her he wasn't too happy, but about what she couldn't imagine. She wondered at Luke's odd behavior as she and the children walked down the hall. He seemed irritated for no reason whatsoever. Unless . . . unless he truly was jealous.

"Do yer father and uncle argue all the time?" Shannon asked Molly.

"Yeah, but they call it discussing."

"When we discuss like that, Pa gets mad," Toby interjected.

Shannon laughed. *Out of the mouth of bairns.*

THE MEN MOVED into the parlor to finish their conversation.

Luke was surprised at the stab of jealousy he'd felt when his brother had flirted with Shannon. He could never remember being jealous when his wife had been alive. He wondered if he should feel guilty. He poured whiskey into two glasses, handed one to Travis and then took the chair next to his brother. "Now tell me, what is this army you're talking about? What do you think is going to happen?"

"The Texas Revolution has begun, you can bet your bottom dollar on that," Travis stated. "It started with a single cannon blast in Gonzales. Don't know how long it'll go on, but Santa Anna will not go away without a fight and, probably, a nasty fight, at that."

Luke nodded. "I agree. It's time for independence. Our numbers have grown in Texas."

"Yep," Travis agreed, looking at the amber liquid in his glass. "We outnumber the Mexican settlers."

"I've heard Santa Anna's army is looting and burning. That's all we need," Luke stood, then walked over to the window before continuing, "It's been bad enough fighting off the Comanche."

"It makes you wonder why we want to live here," Travis grumbled. "I don't expect you to leave the children, but I thought you'd want to know what's happening."

"Of course, I want to know." Luke digested the information. "Maybe, I should hire a few more men for protection. Of course most have volunteered for the army, so finding trustworthy men has been tough."

"I can imagine," Travis said nodding. "At least, you solved one of your worries. You found a nanny."

Luke swung back from the window and slugged down his drink. "She goes back next week."

Travis gaped at him as if Luke had lost his mind. "And why is that? She didn't run out the first week, and that, in itself, is a miracle. You know how many others you've tried."

"She's too young. I advertised for someone older, and she lied to get the job."

"Like you've never told a lie," Travis shot back, then he smiled. "She's what . . . a little younger than Ruth?"

Luke nodded and sat down. "But she's even smaller than Ruth. I don't want to watch Shannon die, too."

"Are you sure that's what the problem is?" Travis asked, determined not to let the subject drop. He knew his brother well. "I don't think so. You're afraid to have someone so tempting around you," Travis got up and poured himself another drink. "For Christ's sake! It isn't right that you're alone, Luke. It's been three years."

"I know how long it's been," Luke snapped, his mouth

thinning with displeasure. "You don't know what it's like to love someone then lose her."

"You're right, I don't," Travis stated then took an abrupt step toward him, "but I do know that when I first saw you tonight, it was the first time in a long time you looked like you were alive again . . . the brother I used to know." Travis leaned toward his brother. "Life goes on. If it doesn't, you might as well have climbed into that hole with Ruth."

Luke leapt to his feet and held up a hand to silence Travis. "Mind your own damned business!" He slammed his glass on the table. "As you said, you've never loved anyone. I'll see you in the morning."

That's all Luke needed, he thought as he strode out. His damned nosy brother giving him advice, the brother who'd never stayed long in one place. The one always looking for adventure and another woman.

How would Travis know what it felt like to love someone and then have them jerked out of your life? And the guilt . . . there was always the guilt for bringing his wife to this savage land.

As soon as the back door slammed and the cool air surrounded Luke, he could feel some of the tension ease out of his shoulders. He breathed in the cool night air. Winter was just around the corner. They might have a few more warm days ahead but summer was gone. This meant he'd be spending more time in the house with his lovely nanny.

Then again, maybe not.

The stage would be back in Cottonwood two days from now. His original plans were to put Shannon back on the stage; however, now that these battles were taking place, he needed to ride with his brother to see what he could do to help. After all, he didn't want to be ruled by Mexican government. Texas needed her freedom, and he needed to do his small part.

Did he dare leave his children with Shannon? He smiled as he thought of how she had tamed them, something the other nannies had not been able to do. The children were different now, and he liked their behavior so much better than when they were running wild. He'd even bet that the kids liked Shannon more than they let on. And he had to admit, he trusted her. She was sweet and caring, and beautiful.

Luke sighed. He couldn't decide what to do about Shannon. Would she be able to survive Texas's harsh winters? Or would she get sick and die as his wife had, leaving the children and him alone again? Then he'd have two deaths haunting him. Luke rubbed the back of his neck. Making decisions had never been a problem in the past. Why was he having so much trouble now?

Letting his hands fall to his sides, Luke glanced up at the full moon. It bathed everything he owned, everything he was proud of building up from nothing. Having worked so hard, Luke wondered if it had been worth it. If he'd stayed back in St. Louis, Ruth might still be alive and his life would be so very different than it was today.

But what life?

He'd have a position in her father's bank being bored out of his mind. He needed wide open spaces, the sun on his face and the wind in his hair.

He'd always heard that God moved in mysterious ways – now he wondered where he was heading with his life. He couldn't go on as he'd been doing. He was tired, and for a brief moment he wondered what it would be like to be like his brother and not have a care in the world. A shadow of annoyance crossed his face and he sighed . . . that wasn't who he was.

Maybe things would look different in the morning.

Instead of going back in the house, Luke decided to look over his new stallion which Wilson had put in the corral earlier today. As he shuffled toward the corral, Luke couldn't seem to get his brother's words out of his head. He hated to admit it. Travis had been right about him. Luke had been living like a dead man.

He worked. He slept. Then he got up the next morning and started all over again. He didn't think he had been capable of feeling anything until Shannon had walked, no stormed, into his life. With that thought, he smiled for the first time today, and a bit of tension seeped out of his body.

When the corral came into view, Luke stopped. For there standing on the fence clinging to the top rail like a child was the object of his thoughts. He had to admit Shannon was like a breath of fresh air.

Her fiery red hair smoldered in the moonlight and reminded him of low-burning embers. His body hardened and that disgusted him. He might be a man but he should have better control over his emotions. He was no better than one of his bulls.

"How do you like my new horse?"

Shannon swung around a little surprised to find Luke walking up behind her, "Hello. Hope ye dinna mind me lookin' at yer horse? He's beautiful."

She turned back to face the pen, grabbing the top rail with her arms. "Look how proudly he holds his head, but I believe he's a bit shy. Canna get him tae come tae me."

"I bet he's the first male you've not been able to charm," Luke commented wryly.

Surprised by his off-handed comment, Shannon climbed down from the railing then turned and leaned against the fence before she spoke. Luke was hard on the outside, but she'd bet if she could break through his protective shell, she'd like what she found. "Canna say I've done tae well with his master."

Luke propped his boot on the rail next to her and leaned on his knee. "Maybe better than you know."

Shannon couldn't believe it, Luke was flirting with her! "Yer in a strange mood tonight," she said with a smile. "Ye want tae talk about it? I'm a good listener."

"It's just that . . ." he paused, "you're not what you seem."

Shannon wasn't sure what she'd expected him to say, but it most certainly wasn't that. "Yer disappointed in me."

"Of course not," he answered quickly. "Well, maybe, at first, because you lied to me. But then, you've actually done very well with the children. At least, they haven't run you off as they did the others." He smiled. His eyes were dark and unfathomable, then he added, "Yet."

"Much to yer disappointment." Shannon laughed. "'Twasn't fer lack of them not tryin'. I believe Molly and Toby are . . . shall we say . . . mischievous. They want attention."

Shannon appeared so pretty in the moonlight, so tempting, Luke thought. Her closeness was like a drug to him. "You might be right," he admitted. "They miss their mother."

"And their father."

Luke reached out and touched her face. Feelings he thought long dead roared to life. He struggled to hold himself back as his fingers slid down the side of her face to rest under her chin, tilting it up so he could see into her eyes. "Why did you come barreling into my life?"

A strange inner excitement filled Shannon and her skin

tingled where he touched her. He was strong and rugged, yet his touch was gentle. Isn't this what she wanted? Could he one day love her? "Because you needed me," she whispered.

"I guess I did." As his warm breath brushed her cheek, he lowered his mouth to hers. Just before kissing her, he murmured in a husky voice, "I really shouldn't be doing this."

"Aye," Shannon agreed as she gazed at him from beneath flirtatiously lowered lashes. "Unless ye want to." The way Luke looked at her made her knees go weak. She couldn't deny this deep compelling attraction she felt for him. And kissing Luke was a rash and reckless thing to do, but necessary if she was going to seduce her cowboy. She'd found what she wanted. She had to make him want her.

With a smothered moan, Luke's arms tightened around her as his mouth opened hungrily over hers. He coaxed her lips open, then his tongue plunged inside her mouth creating the most luscious feeling Shannon had ever felt.

Her arms moved around his neck. She clung to Luke, caressing the back of his neck in slow lazy circles as she enjoyed the kiss. She became lost in a swirl of emotions. Shannon had heard her sisters talking about men and kissing, but she had never thought it could be so wonderful. . . so pleasurable. Most certainly the few kisses she had experienced in England were so formal that they were non-existent compared to this.

Luke pulled back and gazed at her. She could tell he felt something for her, whether he wanted to or not.

"I'm sorry. I shouldn't have done that," he finally said.

"Ye dinna enjoy it?"

Luke looked at her as if she'd said something stupid. "Of course I did." He sighed. "More than you know."

"Well, I'll no apologize for carin' for ye, Luke Griffin."

"Oh, Shannon, if only life were so simple," he murmured then released her. "You can't stay out here."

"I can if ye want me."

"I—I," Luke paused, shook his head, then headed for the barn. "Go back to the house, Shannon," he called over his shoulder, but she also heard him say to himself. "I don't know what I want."

Shannon watched Luke's back and shook her head. She could feel her heart fluttering. That was one forevermore stubborn cowboy. Would he ever be able to let his wife's memory go? Tears stung her eyes as she realized that she'd come to love Luke and his children . . . difficult as they were. What would she do if he sent her away?

8

*A*ll night long Shannon tossed and turned, her mind still on Luke.

Would he send her away now that he knew she was a temptation? Would he treat her coldly in the morning?

He seemed to have enjoyed the kiss as much as she had. Luke was a wonderful kisser. He made her feel things she'd never felt before. And in that one unguarded moment, she saw that he felt the same as she did. A small sigh slipped out.

Oh how she wished she had one of her sisters to talk to. They would know what to do.

Longing to be with her sisters, Shannon began to dream about the last time she'd seen them. They had just come to America . . .

~

SHANNON, Brooke and Jocelyn stood on the rolling deck of the Flying Lady, watching the American shoreline grow bigger, wondering what adventure awaited them.

Shannon, with her romantic notions, believed there was someone out there just for her, preferably a cowboy.

Brooke who didn't believe in love said, "From what I've seen men and women use each other to get what they want. If you don't have money, you have to depend on others. I'm going to make something of my life, and there isn't a man alive I'll let stand in my way." That was Brooke — determined. The strong one.

Once Brooke had told Shannon that as a young girl she'd had visions of true love dancing in her head, but they were soon dashed in the harsh light of reality. Sometimes life didn't turn out liked you hoped.

Now Shannon could agree.

And then there was her real cousin Jocelyn who had met Brooke at boarding school. Jocelyn didn't believe in love either. Unfortunately, of the three of them, she'd tasted love and what had it gotten her? A broken heart and tossed out of her father's house. So she'd turned to her uncle, Jackson Montgomery, and he had taken her into his home where she was reunited with Brooke.

After Jackson Montgomery, Duke of Devonshire, entered Brooke's life, everything had changed. He understood that she wasn't living the life she wanted. Whoever started out wanting to be a courtesan?

It was true that he'd kept Brooke in a townhouse he'd bought just for her, but Jackson wasn't like the other men. She'd told them that he had been her friend, never as much as hinting at sexual relations. It seemed as though in some strange way, he saw the good in Brooke and wanted to protect her. When he'd taken in his nieces, Jocelyn and herself, who were very close to Brooke's age, they had become a family of sorts as the girls had bonded with each other and became sisters with Brooke as the older bossy sister.

Jackson had promised that he'd leave Brooke and the girls well taken care of. So, when he'd died, he'd left Brooke Moss Grove, his American plantation, and enough money for the young women to leave England and make a fresh start in America. Shannon and Jocelyn had wanted no part of the plantation. He also left the incomparable Mr. Jeffries, the solicitor in charge of his affairs, to help the women travel and get settled.

They had been standing by the ship's rail when Shannon shook Brooke's arm, bringing her back from her musings. "Where is Mr. Jeffries?" Shannon paused, then added. "Ye seem tae be daydreamin' a lot lately."

Brooke had given her a faint smile. "I was remembering Jackson. He was such a special and extraordinary man."

"And a good uncle," Jocelyn added.

"As for Jeffries," Brooke said, "I've not seen him since breakfast. He told me that he had to make preparations for our travel to New Orleans."

"Wasn't it grand of Mr. Jeffries to accompany us from England?" Jocelyn turned and propped her arms on the rail. "I'm not sure any of us would have known what to do. We would probably still be standing on the docks in London, watching the ship sail away without us."

"Now, now," Brooke countered. "Somehow, we would have found the correct ship. However, it was Jackson's instructions that Mr. Jeffries would accompany us, so he had no choice. Jeffries told me I had inherited a plantation, and we were provided enough money for travel. And, of course, each of you were left a thousand pounds to help get started. I believe Jackson was hoping we'd all go to Moss Grove. Evidently, he didn't know just how independent his nieces are." Brooke smiled. "But for some strange reason, Jeffries was instructed not to read the entire will until we reached Moss Grove Plantation."

"'Tis a bit odd," Shannon said.

"I thought so, too," Brooke agreed. "The only reason I can

come up with is that it will be easier for me if Jeffries introduces me to the household staff, and to be truthful, I'm glad we have him along.

"America is a strange country I've only read about. I'd be completely lost without him. However," Brooke said with a saucy smile, "I have studied books on the planting of cotton so that I'll know something about living on a plantation."

"I agree." Shannon nodded. "The mon has been verra helpful wi' makin' arrangements fer my trip." Her face lit up with a smile. "Just think, I'm goin' tae be a governess fer two bairns. From their descriptions, they sound adorable."

Brooke looked at Shannon with a look of amused wonder. "Besides being a child yourself, what do you know about children?"

"Verra little," Shannon admitted and then smiled. "I ken if I can handle men and their childish ways, then the bairns wull only be smaller, therefore easier tae handle."

Everyone laughed, enjoying each other's company as they usually did. However, Shannon felt a twinge of sadness, knowing that their time together was slipping away.

"If you ask me, it sounds as if you're going out into the wilderness," Jocelyn said to Shannon.

"Aye, Texas wull be verra different, but different is what I want," she said with a slight smile. "I want adventure and tae see all those cowboys close up."

A loud thump made all three women flinch and grab for the rail as the ship bumped, then settled next to the wooden platform. They peered over the railing, witnessing the dock spring to life with crewmembers racing along the platform, grabbing the ropes to tie off the ship, and shouting instructions to the other shipmates.

The streets leading up to the pier were filled with wooden pier drays, wagons and fruit vendors, each hawking their wares for *money. Wagons lined up waiting for the ship's cargo to be offloaded. And there were a multitude of carriages waiting for disembarking passengers.*

"Do you have your trunk packed?" Brooke asked.

Both women nodded.

"In that case I had better go and get my reticule," Brooke said, turning away from the rail. "I'll meet both of you on the dock."

Slipping her arm through Jocelyn's, they walked down the gangplank to where Mr. Jeffries stood. He had secured a carriage for Brooke and a hack for Shannon and Jocelyn, and he was presently overseeing the loading of their trunks on top of the carriage. Jeffries wasn't a tall man, but he was a couple of inches taller than Brooke. His hair, what there was of it, was gray. He had a bald spot on the very top and bushy hair around the sides. As always, he was dressed in his gray vest and white shirt.

"Miss Shannon and Miss Jocelyn, he acknowledged as Brooke joined them. "I have secured hotel rooms for you at the Block House and have established accounts for both of you at the First National Bank in New York, so funds will be available for you to draw upon."

"How did the money get there?" Brooke asked.

"His Grace had me come to America before his death and make arrangements. I believe he overheard your conversations of wanting to come to America.

"Now, I'll leave you to your goodbyes. Do remember I'll be in this country for a good six months, so if you need me send a wire to Moss Grove, Brooke will know how to get in touch with me."

Shannon and Jocelyn smiled their thanks, then each of them gave him a hug.

"Hear, hear. We'll have none of that," Jeffries blustered. "It's my job, after all."

The women wrapped their arms around Brooke, and she

hugged them back, fiercely holding them to her heart. Shannon knew they were the only family that Brooke had.

"'Tis only goodbye for a wee bit," Shannon whispered. She managed a choked and desperate laugh, tears sliding down her cheeks. "Dinna make me cry. Let's promise that we'll meet in one year at Moss Grove."

"That's an excellent idea," Jocelyn agreed as she brushed the hot, salt tears from her cheeks.

Brooke attempted to give them a brave smile, but her teary eyes betrayed her, as well. "Do you both promise to come? No excuses?"

"We promise."

"Good," Brooke said, nodding with finality. "And you must write often so I'll know how both of you are doing. I promise I'll do the same."

Jocelyn nodded. "Then it's time for us to go."

Since there was nothing left to say, the two women climbed into the hack. "You're going to miss my nagging," Brooke called to them, her voice cracking slightly.

SHANNON STRETCHED her arms over her head, then she folded back the sheet and finally opened her eyes. Her pleasant memories of her sisters had cheered her up, but they faded away with the morning light. Goodness, it seemed like yesterday she'd stood on that ship, but then in the same sense, it also seemed long ago as she was in a different part of the country. Nothing like the sea and the hustle and bustle of the docks.

It was almost as if her sisters were her dream life. She missed them, but she did not regret seeking her own adventure. Shannon didn't know Brooke's address but she would definitely write to Jocelyn.

Of course, she could be heading back to Jocelyn if things didn't go well this morning with Luke. That thought made Shannon very uneasy. She let out a small sigh as she threw back the covers.

Well, she wasn't going to sit in her room and cower. It wasn't in her nature now that she'd left her da. She never wanted to be frightened again.

She would dress and then ask to speak with Luke first thing this morning. Moving to her wardrobe, she couldn't help smiling at her ball gowns, the ones that would never see the light of day out here. She really didn't miss the balls she'd attended in England because she had always felt like she was on display, waiting on a wealthy suitor. That was indeed another life. She doubted that anyone around here knew what a ball was.

Shannon chose a blue, light-weight gown. It had a simple-fitted bodice that opened up the front with tiny pearl buttons and a simple velvet collar.

After laying the dress on the bed she went to the wash-stand and poured water into the basin. She washed her face then picked up her hairbrush and began to remove the tangles from her hair. One of the things she liked about the west is that she didn't have to have her hair fixed every day. She could wear it loose and tied back with a ribbon.

She slipped the dress over her head, letting it fall down over her petticoat. She didn't wear as many petticoats as she used to because they seemed much too impractical for her everyday life now.

Brushing her hands over her dress to smooth out the few wrinkles, she gave one last look in the mirror, straightened her hair ribbon, then nodded her approval. She wanted to find Luke as soon as possible to get this over and done with. She didn't like uncertainty.

Shannon didn't have to go far. She collided with Luke just outside her door. Had he been standing there preparing to knock on the door?

"Ouch." Shannon took a step back. "Just the person I wanted tae see. I'd like tae speak with ye this mornin'.."

"What a coincidence," Luke said. "I want to talk to you, also. Let's go to my office."

Shannon followed him down the hallway. A cordial greeting would have been nice. Like "good morning, how are you"? Any gentleman would have done so. However, she'd already learned she wasn't dealing with a gentleman. She was dealing with a cowboy who was a puzzle to her.

Once they entered Luke's office, which was two doors down from his bedroom, he said, "Have a seat."

She sat in a chair facing the desk while he closed the door. *This couldn't be good,* she thought with a small flutter in her stomach.

"I think we need to discuss last night," Luke said as he turned and leaned back on his desk.

Nothing like getting straight to the point, Shannon thought. "Would ye like me tae pack?"

For just a moment, Luke knew he must appear stunned because he was astonished by his own behavior, but he hadn't realized that he'd upset Shannon so much she wanted to leave. "I didn't mean to upset you." His dark brows slanted in a frown. "I just lost control . . . something that shouldn't have happened. I'm sorry."

"I'm not upset, nor am I sorry we kissed," she admitted. She lifted her chin, meeting his gaze straight on. "However, I am disappointed that ye're sorry."

Luke rubbed his chin. There was something about

Shannon that made her more interesting and intriguing each time he saw her. And he wasn't sure what to do about it. For now he wanted to do the right thing, even if it killed him.

"I thought I had upset you."

"Nay."

He gave her a very puzzled look, and for the first time he realized he truly liked Shannon. "We probably shouldn't be doing . . . well, you know, again." She didn't look convinced. But she was young and naive, and he was older and wiser and knew better. "Now . . ." He leaned on the desk and folded his arms. "I'm going to be leaving for a little while, and I've decided that I want you to stay."

She couldn't believe he had said she could stay. The one thing she'd wanted to hear. But she didn't expect Luke to be leaving, and she was astonished at how he could brush over their kiss. Evidently, it didn't mean as much to him as it had to her. "You're leaving?"

"I'm riding with Travis to see what I can do for this uprising. As you may or may not know, Texas is trying to become independent from Mexico, and I want to do my part. The next battle is close to the ranch and I want to help out."

"I dinna know. Sounds dangerous."

Luke shoved to his feet. "It could be but I'll be all right. However, I need to know that my children will be looked after," he said moving to stand in front of her. "And I think you're the best person for the job." He offered her a hand.

Shannon smiled and placed her hand in his and stood. "Thank ye," she murmured. She stood so close that if she leaned in she could kiss him again, and don't think that wasn't on her mind. Of course, Luke had made it clear their first kiss had been a mistake.

He reached out and touched her face with a gentle caress, and then he straightened and started for the door. "I thought a ride into Cottonwood for supplies would be wise. Would you like to go?"

"I'd love too. Maybe, I can see Emma and Thelma."

Luke swung back with a frown. "I'm sure you will, but why you want to is beyond me. I'll be ready to go in thirty minutes."

"I'll be with ye by then. I want tae write a letter tae my cousin who is probably verra worried about me. I can mail it in town."

"Very well," Luke said.

SHANNON HURRIED to her room and pulled out some stiff cream-colored paper, a quill and a bottle of ink. She sat down and began to compose her letter.

Dear Jocelyn,

I'm sorry I've not written sooner, but the chil-
        dren were a handful when I first arrived.
        Wild would probably be the best word to
        describe them.
Things are finally starting to settle down.
Luke is the cowboy I want. He is everything
        I'd dreamed he'd be. But--and that is a big
        but--he's still in love with his dead wife.
I'm not sure if I can overcome the problem.
        He is, however, starting to show a little
        interest in me, so I'm pleased. Any advice

on how to handle this matter would be
most appreciated. Luke wasn't very happy
that I lied about my age, but he's not
sending me away like he threatened to do
when I first arrived, so I'm making
progress no matter how slow.

Luke does have a fine brother if you're interested. I think the west could appeal
to you.

Can you send me several children's readers?
The children need simple books, and as
I'm in the middle of nowhere they are
hard to come by. And most important,
how are you doing?

Have you found work? I hope by now you
have heard from Brooke. Give her my
address and write soon.

I miss you both and would love to see you.

Love, Shannon

SHANNON SPRINKLED sand on the ink. After grabbing her reticule, she tapped the letter on the desk to remove the sand. Folding the letter she slipped it into the envelope, hoping that she'd hear from her sister soon. She felt better after writing Jocelyn.

Grabbing her cream-colored shawl, she slipped the letter into her pocket and headed for the door. The thought of seeing her traveling mates, Emma and Thelma would be a real treat since they never had company out here. However, it seemed Luke was not too fond of the outspoken sisters. And she wondered why. Perhaps, she'd find out once they reached town.

9

*T*he midmorning sun was bright and the air crisp.
Apparently, they had had their first frost last night, so Shannon was glad to have her heavy wrap as she rushed outside to find the buckboard ready.

Luke, Travis and the children stood beside the wagon along with a couple of brown and chestnut saddle horses. The children wore heavy coats and their cheeks were tinged a lovely shade of pink.

"Appears everyone is waitin' fer me," Shannon said as she slowed her footsteps, remembering that ladies shouldn't run.

"Never did mind waiting for a pretty lady," Travis said smoothly, shoving away from the wagon and gathering his mount's reins.

Shannon smiled at the compliment, keenly aware of Luke's scrutiny as well as the children. As a matter of fact, the children looked as if they had been sucking on lemons.

"And what seems tae be troublin' ye two?"

"Pa said we have to stay with you," Molly pouted.

Shannon gave them a knowing nod. She'd expected that

they wouldn't like the idea of their father leaving them. "I'm sure he explained..." She exchanged a subtle look with Luke,"...that he needs tae be ridin' out with yer uncle. And I'm also sure ye dinna want him tae feel bad aboot that?"

"W--Well no," Molly said, casting her gaze down. "But we'll be staying with *you*."

"And the problem with that bein'?"

"You're mean."

"Am I now?" Shannon chuckled and crossed her arms. "Only when the two of ye force me tae be, and the word is strict, not mean. Therefore as long as ye both behave, I dinna see that ye huv a problem."

By the expression on their faces the children couldn't think of a reply, so they solemnly regarded their father who seemed to be trying to stifle a grin. Were they hoping for contradiction or confirmation? Didn't matter, Shannon supposed.

Luke took Shannon's hand and guided her close to the wagon. "Climb up next to Wilson, and we'll ride along with you," Luke instructed, helping her onto the wagon.

Molly followed, seating herself next to Toby in the back of the wagon. Once they were settled Wilson chucked his tongue to the horses and they ambled forward.

The ride into town was actually a refreshing change of pace. It might be a cold day, but with the sun shining brightly, she barely noticed the cool air. Scotland was cold, but Texas was merely cool. This really was a desolate land yet in an odd sort of way beautiful, for it held the promise of what could be. The cluster of trees here and there added color to the vast brown landscape.

When she had her fill of the scenery, she began watching Luke. He and Travis rode just ahead of the wagon beside the horses. Luke was such a commanding figure. Oh, how she would love to be held in his strong arms and see love in his eyes. But Shannon knew that wouldn't happen overnight. At least Luke hadn't sent her away. She couldn't help thinking that was a small start, and after last night, she did think he was beginning to feel something for her.

As they entered Cottonwood, Shannon snapped out of her musings. The frontier town wasn't like any of the cities she knew in England. To start with, it was very small. After spending a month at the ranch, even tiny Cottonwood was a welcome sight, and she would get to see her friends, Thelma and Emma. The wagon lumbered down the dirt street. They passed the undertaker, the blacksmith shop, and the boardinghouse where she and Luke had eaten dinner.

Across the street, the dry goods store was a clapboard building with a sloping tin roof which covered the boardwalk out front. There were two hitching posts along with a watering trough for the horses. At the top of the building sat a big white sign that read –- *Miller's Dry Goods. If we don't have it . . . you don't need it.*

The buckboard stopped in front of the store, and everyone scrambled out of the wagon and followed Luke. A bell tinkled over head when the door opened. They stepped inside. Thelma stood behind the counter tallying up a stack of receipts while Emma dusted shelves beneath the front window.

The store was crammed full of just about everything, Shannon thought, like the sign said. It had a cozy feel and a variety of merchandise from jars of candy to barrels of nails. There were bolts of colorful fabric, a pickle barrel and picks and shovels.

"Land sake, Emma, look who's come to see us!" Thelma screeched upon seeing Shannon.

"Shannon dear, it's so good to see you," said Thelma

taking Shannon's hand. Thelma whispered, "I see you've survived."

Shannon smiled. "Aye."

"Tell me you've come to get a wedding dress," Emma piped up.

"Wha--?" Shannon sputtered, glancing quickly at Luke. "They--they thought--thought we were getting married."

Luke's expression wasn't very flattering, Shannon thought. He looked like he'd smelled something really foul. Finally, he asked, "What gave you such a fool notion, Emma?"

"Just figured you'd want to do right by Miss Shannon."

"I have done right by her. I've given her a place to stay and my children to look after."

Shannon noticed the "said children" were in the corner of the store with their uncle, picking out their favorite candy.

Thelma raised her brows. "Now isn't that mighty nice of you," she said sarcastically. "But you know, yourself, how people talk. She's young, and you're young, and well . . . you know . . ."

Shannon could see the muscles tightening in Luke's neck, and she was afraid that he was getting ready to blow his top at the nice, well-intended ladies. Even if they were busybodies, she knew they were looking out for her well-being.

"Then, the townsfolk don't have a whole lot to do," Luke finally ground out, ending the discussion. "Here." He handed his list of supplies to Shannon. "You get the supplies. I've got some other things to do."

"My, my, my." Thelma clucked her tongue once Luke had left. "Must have hit a sore spot." She laughed, then added, "Probably one of many."

"I do believe ye did." Shannon agreed as she watched Luke retreat quickly. *However, he dinna huv tae act as if he'd rather hang,* she thought. Shannon swung back around and handed Emma the list. "We need a few supplies." She glanced around. "Where is yer other sister?"

"Afraid Rose is feelin' poorly," said Thelma. "She's just not a spring chicken anymore."

Shannon smiled, thinking what a funny statement for someone who was over seventy and had snow white hair.

Travis brought the children over to the front counter. "I'd like to pay for the children's treats."

"And who are you, young man?" Thelma questioned.

Shannon thought that was a strange question, and what did it matter who he was? He only wanted to purchase something. She saw Travis smile at her confusion. Then he leaned over and whispered, "Small town. They want to know your family history."

"Can't you see the family resemblance?" Travis smiled and tipped his black hat back. "I'm Luke's bother, ma'am."

"Now that you mentioned it." Thelma nodded. "I can see the resemblance; however, I'm not sure I've ever seen your brother smile," she said frankly. "You seem a lot more friendly."

"Why, thank you, ma'am. My brother does have a sorry attitude every now and then."

Thelma handed the children their bags of candy.

"What do ye say?" Shannon prodded.

"Thank you, Miss Thelma and Uncle Travis."

Shannon beamed at the progress the children had made. Those two had come a long way. "Now don't eat it all at once."

"But it's ours," Toby protested.

Well maybe they had a little farther to go in the manners department, Shannon thought.

"Aye. But if ye eat all that candy ye'll huv a tummy ache fer sure."

"Oh, all right," Molly said grudgingly. She sucked on a horehound drop as they left the store with Travis.

"There are some fine men in that family." Emma sighed. "If only I were a bit younger."

Shannon laughed. She really would have liked to have known these two when they were younger. "While I'm thinking aboot it," she paused, "do ye huv any books for *bairns*?"

"*Bairns*?" Thelma asked.

"Children," Shannon clarified.

"Afraid not, honey. Not many children around here can read. We don't even have a school teacher."

Emma peered over her glasses at Shannon. "You know, there was a man in here the other day who talked the same way you do. We thought it strange to have met two Scots way out here."

For a moment, Shannon couldn't say anything. She felt a hot, queasy feeling spread through her. *'Twas very strange*, she thought. And probably no coincidence, either. What was she going to do if her father's men had found her?

"Are you all right, dear?" Thelma said, patting Shannon's hand.

"Ah, yes I'm fine. If ye huv everythin' ready." She paused, gesturing toward the boxes of groceries and bags of grain. "I'll find Luke so he and Travis can load the supplies, Shannon said in more or less a daze as she turned to leave. "Be back in a moment."

Resisting the urge to run, Shannon hurried for the door.

She stepped outside and blinked a couple of times as her eyes adjusted to the sunlight. Suddenly, she felt as if she were suffocating. It brought back all the old feelings she used to have when she was around her da. Perhaps, the sisters were mistaken and only thought they heard a Scottish accent. Maybe it was British instead, she thought hopefully.

She glanced around for the children or Luke, but didn't see anyone she knew, so she sauntered down the sidewalk a little ways, then a door opened across the street and caught her attention.

She stopped.

Shannon saw Luke stepping from the boardinghouse followed by Louise. His back was to Shannon as he talked to the woman. Not only talking -- he was holding her hand. Shannon wanted to cry, yet she knew she had no right. Still, she didn't like seeing Luke with another woman, especially one that made him laugh. How many times had she seen him laugh? She could probably count the times on one hand.

Yet she couldn't take her eyes off Luke, and that is why she didn't see or hear the man coming up behind her.

The next thing she knew a man's arm had snaked about her waist, pinning her to him. "Wull if it isn't Shannon McKinley in the flesh, and she's finally alone."

At the sound of his voice, Shannon's blood ran cold.

"I ken yer da wull be mighty glad tae see ye," he said, his mouth close to her ear.

"Let me go," Shannon said through gritted teeth, trying to keep a cool head. But the man was pulling her down the empty sidewalk, and so far he'd not attracted any attention. A little further and they would be at the alley, and she knew what that meant. Shannon bit the man's hand across her mouth, then let out a blood curdling scream when he jerked his palm away.

He reacted by jerking her around and striking her hard across the face, knocking her to the ground. Then he yanked her back up, slapped his hand back over her mouth as he dragged her toward the alley. She struggled, kicking out at him with her feet and trying to break free from his hold. Nothing seemed to be working.

They had just reached the mouth of the alley when a voice sliced through the air. "Let the woman go!"

Suddenly, they stopped moving. Her assailant swung her around to face the boardwalk behind them, and she saw Luke standing at the edge of the alley.

"I said, let her go!" Luke repeated.

"What's it tae ye?"

"She belongs to me. And if you don't let her go, I'm going to blow your brains out."

Shannon felt her assailant tense as he considered the options. His arm around her tightened, then he took another step back further into the alleyway.

"If ye come any closer, I'll kill her," he warned, and then he took two more steps backward using Shannon as a shield. Would Luke take the chance and stop this brute? She didn't see how as she was directly in the line of fire.

The man holding Shannon drew out his gun and pressed it against her back. She could feel the barrel as he moved to get a bead on Luke. Luke wouldn't have a chance to draw. But before Shannon could yell, she felt herself being thrown to the side, her head hitting the wall.

Gunfire exploded.

Shannon's ears buzzed from the sound of the blast, and it took a moment before she could push herself up off the ground. She was so woozy. Vaguely, she saw Travis ushering the children out of the eating-house. She hoped they hadn't seen what had happened.

And there in the dirt, lying face down was her assailant. Groping the wall, she attempted to stand, but her trembling legs wouldn't support her.

Luke grabbed her before she slumped back down. "Are you all right?" he asked, his eyes taking in every detail. He touched the red spot on her cheek.

"I-I'm fine. I think," said Shannon weakly.

"Here." Luke moved her next to the wall. "Prop against the wall so I can get a good look at this piece of shit."

He pushed the dead man over with the toe of his boot as Travis came running up to them.

"Where are the children?" Luke asked.

"With Thelma and Emma," Travis said. "What in the hell happened?"

"Don't know," Luke snapped. "This sidewinder was man-handling Shannon. I intended to wound him, but it didn't work out liked I'd planned. Maybe you should get the sheriff, Travis."

Luke searched the dead man's shirt and found a wallet. After he thumbed through the contents, he paused, pulled a paper from the wallet, then moved back over to Shannon. He noticed that she had a small knot coming up on her forehead.

"Do you know this man?"

"Nay, I've never seen him before."

"Strange," Travis said, his brow raised. "He comes from your neck of the woods. His name is Alasdair McKinley. A relative?"

"Nay. I just told ye I've never seen him. Our clan was large and I dinna know everyone."

"Really?" Luke's tone was sarcastic. "Then why would he

have this drawing of you," he snapped and shook the paper at her, "with a damn good description?"

Luke watched the color drain from Shannon's face, and he knew she wasn't telling him everything. What was she hiding? A few minutes ago she'd scared the shit out of him. Now he found he wanted to shake the answers from her.

"It wull take a bit o' explainin', but I'd rather not do it in the middle o' the street if ye dinna mind."

Luke finally noticed Sheriff Redick had arrived and onlookers were gathering. "Sheriff, if you don't need me for this, I'm going to return to my family."

"So you don't know him?"

"Nope." Luke shook his head. "Until a few minutes ago, I'd never laid eyes on him. Probably some drifter. He was attacking my nanny and I challenged him. He drew first. I had no choice but to defend myself."

"All right," the sheriff sighed. "I think I can handle it, Luke. Good thing you don't come to town often." The sheriff chuckled. "Every time you do, someone gets killed."

Luke didn't bother to comment. Instead, he went to where Shannon leaned against the wall and lifted her in his arms, then he strode toward the dry goods store. Luke found himself trembling inside now that everything had settled down. He couldn't remember the last time he'd been so scared. He took a deep calming breath. When he'd turned around and saw that brute dragging Shannon into the alley, he'd seen red. He didn't want anyone else touching her.

Such a strange feeling. It was not one he wanted to explore.

They entered the rough-hewn store once more, the bell tinkling overhead. He set Shannon on her feet, but kept an arm around her waist – just in case she proved to still be wobbly.

Immediately, the children ran to Shannon and wrapped their arms around her sobbing. "We thought you were dead," they both cried together.

Luke's heart gave a little lurch. Apparently, his children knew how important Shannon was in their life. That was something he was only just discovering himself. His children had never embraced anyone since their ma died. Strange, how had Shannon made such a difference in such a short time?

Shannon was completely surprised that the little rascals cared. "I'm fine," she said. She tried to lean down to hug them, but she was so dizzy that she managed only to pat them on their backs instead.

"Lands sake," Emma shouted, rushing over to her. "Heard what happened. Let me put something on your head and clean your face while the men load the wagon. Run along children and help your pa."

The next thing Shannon knew, she'd been pulled out of Luke's arms and ushered toward the backroom, and he'd been shooed away. They might be bossy old ladies, but they did seem to care, and she really appreciated their friendship.

Shannon clutched her hands to keep them from shaking now that the worst had passed. The next couple of hours went by in a blur as Emma fussed over her. Emma placed a cold compress on Shannon's head. They also gave her a splash of brandy which they guaranteed would help calm her nerves. It seemed the sisters used brandy all the time to cure their aches and pains. They called it their miracle cure-all.

However, they were right, she did feel much better after her second drink. She'd not had any sprits since England. She felt the warmth spread all over her body as she sipped the smooth liquid. And the third drink tasted better than the first two.

～

CALLUM STOOD behind the saloon holding the two horses while he waited for Alasdair to bring Shannon to him. He'd be glad to have the girl so they could leave this god-forsaken country.

However he wondered what was taking so long and then he heard the gunshot. "Hum, that surely dinna sound good," he mumbled. He tied the horses and made his way to the alley just as a group of men strode out.

Callum could see Alasdair lying in the dirt and a dread ran through him. He waited until the Sheriff had walked away. Callum would not leave Alasdair in the dirt like a common animal. Callum went and got the horses and when no one was watching, he tossed Alasdair across the saddle, covered him with a blanket, and hightailed it out of town.

Callum would find someplace to bury his friend, and then he'd watch and wait until he could snatch Shannon. And this time he wouldn't fail.

The lass was going home one way or the other.

10

*A*fter a while, Luke appeared in the back room's doorway and gave Shannon a start of surprise especially as she'd been thinking about him. He looked breathtakingly handsome, as he always did, and a little concerned.

He leaned against the door jamb. "Are you feeling well enough to travel?"

"Aye," Shannon said with a nod and a grin. In spite of her headache, she certainly had lustful thoughts about Luke right this moment. He was a fine mon and when his bold eyes met hers a strange warmth spread over her. Of course, the brandy could have something to do with it, but she didn't think so.

Luke shoved away from the door to help Shannon stand. When he was sure she was steady on her feet, they made their way out of the backroom, slowly walking to the front of the store.

"Thanks fer all yer help," Shannon said, hugging Emma and Thelma goodbye. "I want ye tae come and visit us."

Shannon glanced at Luke to confirm the invitation, and he grudgingly nodded.

Thelma glared at Luke. "You take good care of Miss Shannon. She might still be a little shaky. Land sake, being attacked on our own streets. What's a body to think?"

"I'll take care of her," Luke assured them. "Obliged for your help, ladies."

Outside, Shannon didn't see anything but the buckboard which had been loaded, a tarp spread tight across the top of the supplies. "Where are the children and Travis?"

"Travis and Wilson took the saddle horses and children back to the ranch. I knew you'd need a little more time before you could travel." Luke helped her up on the wagon seat, then placed a blanket over her legs since it was still chilly outside. "It's a little late to be traveling." He glanced up at the darkening sky. "But there will be a full moon tonight to provide us a little light. The roads are fairly straight so we shouldn't have a problem. I also thought we'd have a chance to talk on the way back home."

Once Luke was seated, Shannon glanced at him. "Talk? About what?"

He ignored her. He clucked his tongue, snapped the reins, and the team started forward, clopping along until they were out of town. It brought back memories of her first ride to the ranch.

Of course, then she'd wanted to talk.

They traveled in silence for a little while. She thought maybe Luke had forgotten that he wanted to talk, but as soon as they turned onto the last road toward home, he asked, "Why did that man have your picture?"

Shannon was sure Luke wasn't going to understand; he didn't seem the understanding sort. She bumped her nose with the back of her hand, realizing that it was quiet numb.

She'd much prefer riding along with her leg pressed next to Luke's instead of answering his questions.

She glanced at the setting sun. "'Tis late." Shannon decided to change the subject, avoiding Luke's question all together. "I saw ye talkin' tae Louise. Ye must miss seein' her?"

Luke jerked around. "Miss seeing her? What kind of question is that?"

"I thought ye were courting her before I came?"

"You thought wrong." Luke grumbled. "And you still haven't answered my question."

Shannon couldn't help the little flutter in her stomach. Maybe Luke wasn't in love with the other woman, but he was back on the subject she really didn't want to discuss. Obviously, there was no avoiding it this time.

"I dinna ken who he was," said Shannon finally. She took a deep breath and added, "But I expect he was hired by my da."

Luke glanced at her. "Da?"

"My father if ye want tae call him that because he wasn't much o' one."

Luke frowned as he stared down the dark road, bathed by the last faint rays of light. He handed Shannon the reins. "Don't drop them." He lit a lantern that hung on a pole above their heads. The woman wasn't making much sense, and she seemed to be swaying a lot, much like the lantern. What had those two old biddies given her? "Why would he send someone after you?"

"Probably because I took my mother's jewelry when I left, and he had intentions of marrying me off into a nearby clan so that the McKinley clan would be stronger," Shannon admitted. She had started to tell him about the little bit of money she'd inherited, but that would bring up even more questions she didn't want to answer."

"You're a thief?" he asked in an accusing voice. After all, she was taking care of his children, damn it. He had a right to know about her life.

"Nay. My mother gave me her jewels. She knew I'd need them. So they were mine, but my da dinna see it that way. Ye see, my da killed my mother," Shannon said softly.

Luke listened as she told him about her childhood. Every once in awhile she'd hiccup, which told him the good sisters had given her some hard liquor, no wonder she was swaying. As he listened, he found he wanted to do bodily harm to her so-called father. How any man could treat a woman like that was beyond him.

He glanced at Shannon. Her face was bathed in the soft light of the lantern. *Shannon was in his blood.* The realization struck him so fast that he felt like he'd been slugged. He'd become emotionally involved with Shannon when he'd never planned to keep her in his life.

"Look. There's the ranch up ahead," Luke said. It was late and he was glad to see the lights. He felt like a sitting duck on this buckboard, and his mind was starting to drift in dangerous directions where Shannon was concerned. "I'm glad you left under those circumstances, and it was nice of your uncle to take you in for a short while. Do you suppose your father will send someone else for you?"

"Nay, the mon must be running out of money. But then desperate men do desperate things, so 'tis possible he sent a couple of men," she added.

Luke pulled the wagon to a halt. A couple of ranch hands came running out, but not Wilson, which Luke thought was strange. Maybe his foreman was busy elsewhere. Luke issued orders for everything to be unloaded before he escorted a swaying Shannon into the house.

"Señor Luke," called Maria in a nervous sort of way. "Señor Travis and Wilson took the children to Señor George. Señor Travis said to tell you they would be back in two days," she told him as she wrung her hands. "I told him he needed to wait for you, but he said you wouldn't mind."

Shannon was leaning against Luke, and he knew she wouldn't last much longer on her feet. The problem was every time she moved; her breast rubbed against him, producing a delicious heat he couldn't do a damn thing about.

He took a deep breath. What in the Sam Hill was his brother thinking? Running off to their brother George's house without asking first. Travis was too damn carefree for his own good. However there was no need taking out his displeasure on Maria. "It's all right, Maria. I'll deal with Travis when he returns."

"What happen to Señorita Shannon?"

"Hello, Maria," Shannon said, her words slurred.

"She's had a slight accident and received a nasty bump on her head," Luke explained as he tightened his grip on Shannon. "It's late. Why don't you go on to bed. I'll see Miss Shannon to her room."

Maria nodded. "*Sí*, if you're sure."

"I'm sure. It's been a long day for all of us."

Once Maria had left, Luke helped Shannon down the hall. She seemed to be leaning on him more and more. He nudged her again. "Are you awake?"

"Aye. Just a wee bit sleepy. How about ye?"

"I'm a little tired myself."

Luke shoved open the door to Shannon's room.

Someone had already lit a lamp. Her bed was covered in clothes and shoes. "This is where you sleep?"

"I was in a bit o' a hurry this mornin'." She waved her hand toward the bed. "'Tis a bit messy. Did Maria say the children are gone?"

"She did. Travis took them to my older brother's."

"Ye never said anythin' about a brother living out here."

"I don't see much of him," Luke said. He was going to have Shannon stand while he cleaned off the bed, but the minute he let her go she swayed.

"This isn't going to work. Come on," he turned her around. "You can sleep in my bed and then I'll come back and clean yours off."

"I like yer bed," Shannon murmured. "'Tis softer than mine."

Those few words sent heat roaring through Luke much like a wildfire consuming the prairie. He wanted this woman, no matter how much he tried to deny it. Her smile warmed his heart even if he didn't want it to.

They made their way down the hall and into his wing. He bumped the door with his shoulder then leaned down and swung Shannon up into his arms and carried her over to the big bed where he deposited her.

However . . . she didn't remove her arms and Luke knew he was in *real* trouble now.

"Ye do that verra well," Shannon murmured.

He ran a forefinger over her smooth cheek. "So I've been told."

His face was so close, and she wanted him so badly, so why not kiss him? She was afraid and intrigued at the same time. She didn't want her heart broken. She had seen how badly her cousin Jocelyn had been hurt. But on the other hand, why not satisfy the longing she had deep within her?

The cowboy she had always wanted. Wasn't Luke what she'd longed for? She felt passion racing through her, clouding her brain. "Kiss me," she whispered.

"You don't know what you're saying," Luke told her.

"I know exactly what I'm saying and exactly what I want," said Shannon feeling much more alert than she had a moment ago. She was dismayed at the magnitude of her desire. She pulled his head down to hers.

It was the only encouragement Luke needed.

A groan of surrender sounded just before his warm lips brushed back and forth across her ear. Shannon realized that he was giving her a chance to back away, but she didn't want to. He whispered in her ear, "Are you sure?"

Shannon's heart fluttered as she nodded. His tongue traced each curve of her ear, giving her delicious shivers and his warm breath was producing a desire so strong that she was only aware of Luke . . . his strength. . . his body.

She moved beneath him, causing him to make a deep sound of male pleasure. His hot lips found hers and in that moment Shannon knew she'd found heaven. Desire flooded her body with warmth she'd never experienced as she drank in the sweetness of his kiss.

Luke pulled back slightly and unfastened the buttons on her blouse, then pushed it open. "Beautiful," he murmured as he stared down at her so intently that Shannon's skin burned. His hand moved over her breast, but that didn't seem to satisfy him. He grabbed her chemise at the neck and tore the thin material exposing both her breasts.

She gasped as the cool air hit her bare skin.

He caressed her nipples until they tightened, and then his mouth replaced where his fingers had been. He was so tender that she cried out as she felt the flaming touch of his swirling tongue. Desire was an emotion she'd never truly experienced but now that she had, she wanted more. She wanted to say something but no words came to her. She pressed against him, a small moan slipped passed her lips.

Luke raised up on his arms and looked at her with such passion that her heart gave a small jump. She wanted him to feel the same pleasure that she was feeling. She fumbled with the buttons on Luke's shirt until she finally got it opened. Rubbing her hands across his chest, she marveled at the ripples of his hard muscles and the thicket of dark hair. She rubbed his hard nipples and felt him jerk when she touched him. Shannon liked the thought that she could make him desire her.

Her hands slid into Luke's hair and pulled him back to her breast. His tongue tantalized her nipples, which were swollen to their fullest. She felt moisture between her legs and knew there was something more.

Luke slipped from the bed. She looked longingly at him as he disposed of the rest of his clothing, leaving her a full view of a well-muscled body. Then he was back on the bed and with a flick of his hand he'd removed her remaining clothing, exposing all of her to him.

"I want you so damn bad," Luke admitted, an admission Shannon sensed he had struggled with. "I shouldn't, but I do."

Again Shannon couldn't talk. All she could do was hold her arms up to him. He joined her and immediately she felt the heat of his body and a hardness between her legs that made her gasp.

He traced a line between her lips with his tongue. The moment she yielded, his tongue plunged into her mouth, stroking and caressing, communicating with unspoken words. Her senses skidded out of control.

God, how he wanted her. Luke knew he should stop, but

when Shannon touched his bare skin, he growled and delved into the warmth of her mouth. His tongue mating with hers as he tasted the sweetness she offered. The degree to which she responded stunned him.

He drew back a little. He'd never wanted a woman the way he wanted Shannon. Staring into her liquid green eyes, dark with desire, he knew he'd never let this woman leave him. It was an awakening experience that left him reeling.

His fingers slid into the soft curls covering the most sensitive part of her and stroked, watching the surprise on her face. Was she as innocent as she seemed?

She moaned his name, and he realized he needed her now. He settled himself between her legs, lifted her hips and plunged inside, finding out only too late that Shannon was very innocent. Her fingernails dug into him as she cried out in pain.

"I'm so sorry I've hurt you," Luke rasped, a lump formed in his throat. "You should have told me."

"Told ye what?"

"That you were a virgin," Luke said as he tried not to move. "Lie still. The pain will ease in a moment."

"I dinna know it would hurt," she whimpered.

"Do you want me to stop?" Luke prayed she didn't.

"Is that all there is?"

Luke couldn't help chuckling. "No, my love. Let me show you," he whispered. Then he started to move again very slowly.

Shannon wasn't too sure about this new experience. Her body was still tense from the pain. No one had ever mentioned pain. This was supposed to be a wonderful experience, but she wasn't too keen on the idea at the moment.

"Take a deep breath and relax," Luke murmured.

Easy for him to say, Shannon thought. But she did as he

instructed and to her surprise the pain wasn't as bad. It was replaced with something else . . . a new feeling. She could only describe it as an itch that needed to be scratched. She wanted something more.

As Luke moved, she began to feel a pressure building inside her, becoming so intense that she tightened her arms around Luke and whispered, "Please." So unsure of what she wanted, but she knew she wanted it now.

Finally a thousand stars exploded from within her and she knew complete contentment as she whispered, "I love you."

---

11

*T*he next morning Luke awoke to a soft body curled against him and a feeling of wonderful contentment coursing through his veins, something he'd not experienced in a long, long time. He wondered about this odd feeling until the events from last night flooded his mind.

And then the guilt settled in.

It was true he desired Shannon – a fact he could no longer deny. However, he was bewildered by his own behavior. What had caused him to act so irrationally when he'd never done so in the past?

Hell, that was a stupid question – it was lust plain and simple – wasn't it? It had to be lust and that wasn't a reason to betray Ruth.

But Ruth was dead.

True, he thought, but he'd loved her dearly. Her death had devastated him. She'd still be alive if he hadn't dragged her to Texas. She had been perfectly happy in St. Louis, but he hadn't. Originally, his family had come from St. Louis. However, once his mother had died, his father and brothers had moved to Texas, and he'd left Ruth behind. He'd never been a city boy. Ruth knew that small fact since they had grown up together.

Luke had found out that he had a wild streak running through him. For two years he'd fought gunfighters not caring if he lived or died. Then a letter from Ruth saying she wasn't going to wait for him any longer woke Luke up so he bought the ranch and went back to St. Louis for Ruth.

Ruth was hesitant at first to move to Texas, but she'd loved him and finally said yes as long as he built her a fine house. Those memories were so long ago they were beginning to fade.

Ruth should be the one lying next to him, then his children wouldn't be without a mother. Would he ever stop feeling guilty?

He had his doubts. Life didn't always turn out the way you planned, and he was now realizing that instead of moving on, he'd retreated into himself. He didn't much like it, but was unsure how to handle the problem.

Luke glanced down at Shannon whose head lay on his arm as she snuggled next to him. He couldn't deny it felt good to hold her, nor could he deny he'd enjoyed making love to her. She was kind of -- how should he put it -- like an old shoe . . . comfortable once you slip it on.

But Shannon had been a virgin. She should have been saving herself for her husband. He took a deep breath, then let it out slowly. Why hadn't she tried to stop him? Had she been hoping to catch herself a husband? Namely him? As the ugly thought crawled into his head, he frowned. Could Shannon be *that* calculating? He wouldn't like to think so, but what did he really know about her?

She had opened up a little on their ride home. He'd thought she'd held something back when he'd first met her and he'd been right. It didn't sound as if her childhood had been pleasant. He also remembered the rage he'd felt toward her father if, indeed, you could call him a father. Did that mean he was starting to care for Shannon?

His head was splitting with so many questions and no answers. However, the biggest question was -- what was he going to do? Luke glanced back down and found that the object of his thoughts had awakened and was gazing up at him. Feelings he considered long dead roared to life, and he struggled to hold himself back. How he'd love to make love to her all over again.

"Good Morning," Shannon said sleepily.

Even though Luke really wanted to kiss her, he wanted the answers to his burning questions more. "Why didn't you stop me last night?" he rasped, realizing he could have been a little more tactful with his question.

Shannon glanced up at him, a puzzled look in her eyes. If she was acting, she was doing a damn good job. Luke thought.

"Was I supposed tae?"

Luke frowned. He pulled away from her and sat up on the side of the bed. "What kind of question is that?" Bending over he snatched his pants off the floor, then jammed his legs into his britches. He was furious with himself. He wasn't someone to lose control. He liked every-thing running smoothly. He ran a hand through his hair in frustration. "Of course you were. You were a virgin, for Christ's sake. You should have been saving yourself for your husband."

Shannon sat up, clasping the cover up to her chin. What the devil had gotten into Luke this morning? He didn't seem to have a problem last night. "Evidently, I dinna bother tae read the rules."

"I'd hate for men to think of you as loose," he said as he snatched his shirt off the floor. "I guess I should marry you."

Shannon felt as if she'd been doused with a bucket of ice water. "How nice of ye tae come tae my rescue! But I dinna believe I've asked for yer help," she retorted indignantly. "I'll only marry for love, nothing less."

"Many marry for convenience."

Having heard quite enough from the lousy lout, Shannon slid out of bed, clutching the covers to her. He'd taken something she'd thought was beautiful and made it feel dirty. She flung the sheet over her shoulder and marched over to stand in front of the insufferable fool.

"Ye get this straight, Luke Griffin. I'm not *many,* ye ken? And I'll not huv yer pity." Shannon's spine stiffened. "As a matter of fact, I canna think o' one thing that I want from ye at this very moment."

"I don't know what you're getting so upset about," Luke roared. "I'm offering you a solution to your problem."

She stiffened. "'Tis mighty noble of ye, but I dinna think there was a problem. Evidently, I've made a mistake, but it's my problem. Now, get out of my way."

She swept by Luke, snatched up her discarded clothes, then hurried to her room before she did anything else that couldn't be undone. She was thankful the children were not at home as she ran through the house to the safety of her room. She needed time to think about what she'd done without distractions.

From the moment she'd first seen Luke, some invisible thread had linked them together – she'd felt it right away. He needed her and she needed him. Yet, when he'd offered marriage –- something she wanted -- Shannon realized she wanted more.

She wanted love.

Could Luke love her? Or did he merely feel lust for her? She sensed he'd felt something last night or maybe it wasn't anything more than lust. She really wished that Brooke was here so she could talk to her and have her questions answered. Shannon sighed. Perhaps, he'd simply forgotten how to love having mourned his wife for so long.

Shannon's head hurt, not to mention the rest of her body. Hoping to ease the ache, she grabbed some clean clothes from her wardrobe and stormed out to take a bath in the children's bathroom.

She paced as the maids filled the tub with hot steaming water. Finally, she was alone. She couldn't help moaning with pleasure as she lowered her body into the warm water. She spotted a smear of blood on her thigh, a small reminder of what she'd done. It took awhile, but finally the tension eased out of her as if someone had pulled a plug.

Of course, her head wasn't going to quit hurting as long as Luke was on her mind, but at least she'd gotten some relief elsewhere. Shannon thought about last night and how bold she'd been. No wonder Luke hadn't considered she might be a virgin.

He had made her feel wonderful and so content that she hadn't considered the consequences. However, Luke's regrets this morning had robbed her of any joy she'd felt. If she were smart, she'd pack her bags and leave right now. It would serve him right. But would he care if she left?

After her bath, Shannon dressed in a brown skirt and a cream-colored blouse and headed for the kitchen.

"Good morning, Maria," Shannon said upon entering the comfortable room.

"Are you hungry, señorita?"

"Starved." Shannon's stomach rumbled to confirm that she was very hungry. "Sorry. Where is Luke?"

"He said he wasn't hungry. Rode out to the north range about an hour ago," Maria said as she pulled a couple of tortillas off the grill. "Seemed to be in a real temper this morning."

Shannon tried not to look disappointed. "Thanks." Shannon said as she took a plate from Maria.

While Shannon ate, Maria continued preparing food for the next meal. They carried on with small talk while Shannon ate, but she had a hard time not thinking about Luke.

"I'm not sure what tae do since the children are away," Shannon admitted. She couldn't remember when she ever felt so lost and unsure of herself.

"Perhaps, you would like to go for a ride and enjoy the outdoors," Maria suggested.

"Aye, that sounds like a lovely idea. Do they huv side-saddles out here?"

"I've not seen any, but I have something that will work for you," Maria said as she hurried from the room.

Shannon took her plate to the sink and washed it while she waited for Maria to return. It would feel good to be outside in the fresh air, riding as she used to do back home.

"I think this will fit you," Maria said holding up a pair of men's trousers. "See, it is split in the middle so that you can ride like a man. Just slip it under your skirt."

Shannon started laughing. "Do women really do this?"

"*Sí*, Señorita Shannon," she said with a smile.

It wasn't far down to the barn which was on the other side of the corral. She could feel her headache easing from just being outdoors. The barn was medium-sized with four stalls on each side. As soon as she entered, she found Ned, who was in charge of the horses.

"I would like tae go ridin', Ned. Will ye saddle a horse fer me?"

"Yes, ma'am." He nodded. "I'd be happy to. I've got a gentle pinto for you," he said grabbing a bridle off the peg. "I've let Molly ride him a couple of times.

Shannon waited by the barn door until Ned brought her mount around. He was white, splashed with brown and a bit smaller than the horses back home.

"Need any help?" Ned asked.

"I think I can manage," Shannon said as she swung up and over the horse. After she'd seated herself, she decided that riding astride was much more comfortable than riding sidesaddle.

It would certainly be easier to keep her balance as she rode. However, if she were in England, Shannon could imagine how the *ton* would frown upon something so unladylike.

"Everything all right?" Ned asked when she hadn't moved. His gray eyebrows were drawn together in a frown. "You do know how to ride?"

Shannon glanced at Ned whose puzzled expression almost made her laugh. "Yes, I'm quite comfortable, although it seems odd when I'm used to riding sidesaddle."

"Sidesaddle?" Ned said. "I ain't never heard of such a thing. Sounds fancy."

"'Tis," she said with a smile. She hesitated before going on. "I huv tae admit that this seems better. Now, can ye tell me the direction where I might find Mr. Griffin?"

"Yesum. Head north. You can't miss him." Ned shoved his hat back. "I see some dark clouds in the distance, so you'd best keep an eye on them. Sometimes storms can move in pretty quick 'round here."

Shannon nodded. She swung her horse around and headed out away from the house. She saw the clouds in the distance but at the moment the sun was still bright, so she figured she'd have plenty of time to catch up with Luke. Besides which, the sun felt good on her back and the wind in her face made her feel young and carefree, something she'd not experienced in a long time.

This land was nothing like the Highlands, she thought as she headed out, but it was beautiful in its own way. She rode toward the herd of cattle scattered across the range in small groups as they grazed, peaceful.

There was wildness about the land that intrigued her. She could see why Luke loved it so much. Was it a place she could call home? She thought so. In spite of Luke's treatment of her this morning, she really felt comfortable here . . . and safe. Luke made her feel safe.

She had been riding for what seemed like ten minutes, when she spotted a group of men working on the fence. Nudging her horse forward with her heels, she raced across the prairie toward them.

"Who the hell is that?" One of the ranch hands said as he straightened.

Wilson turned around. "I do believe that Miss Shannon is coming to call. Nobody could miss that red hair of hers."

Luke stiffened the minute Wilson mentioned red hair. Slowly, he turned around. "What the hell is she doing out here?" He shoved his hat back, then yanked off his leather gloves, as he headed toward her. "Get back to work," he told the men. "The fence won't mend itself."

Luke strode away from the men, realizing that he'd had a

burr under his saddle all day . . . and here she came. He reached Shannon before she got closer to the other men.

She pulled her horse to a halt, and Luke noted that Shannon obviously knew a thing or two about horses. "Is something wrong?" he asked.

"I might ask ye the same thing, the way ye ran from the house this verra mornin'."

"I didn't run," Luke replied. "I had work to do as usual."

"Wull, I want tae discuss last night, if ye please."

"Out here?" His left eyebrow rose a fraction as his gaze locked with hers.

"Not exactly. I-I thought we could go somewhere so we could be alone," Shannon stammered.

Luke nodded. "Wait here." He strode over and retrieved his horse, then motioned for Shannon to follow him, noting that the sky was growing darker. He'd make this a quick chat before the storm let loose.

They rode a short distance away from the ranch hands over to a huge cottonwood tree that would provide some privacy.

"I'm sorry about last night," Luke apologized, not bothering to dismount.

Shannon sighed. "Was I that bad?"

Luke chuckled, wondering how she'd come up with that fool notion. At least, the tension eased out of his shoulders a bit. "What a thing to say. No. You were not bad. That isn't a question a lady should ask, anyway. I'm just sorry about—"

She stiffened the minute he chuckled. "'Twas my choice, but ye needin't feel guilty," she snapped, lifting her chin a tad higher. I could huv said no, but for me it felt verra right."

Luke realized he wasn't handling any of this correctly. "Listen Shannon, it isn't you. It's me. I don't know how to explain–" Hell, he didn't even know how to finish his sentence. He needed to explain that he wasn't laughing at her. But this wasn't a conversation they should be having under a tree, for Pete's sake. Thunder rumbled in the background.

Without warning, lightning struck the backside of the tree they were under, and both horses reared. Luke fought to control his mount, but Shannon's pinto bolted across the uneven ground as a loud crack of thunder split the air.

"Son-of-a-bitch!" Luke swore. His heart lodged in this throat. Frightened from the boom, the steers started to stampede, their sharp horns and large bodies charging toward Shannon. Before he could will her to tug on her reins and veer to the right, her mount jumped a dead log, nearly unseating her. Luke let out another expletive, kneed his mount, and tore out after her.

Another bolt of lightning sent the cattle in a ninety-degree turn so that they were headed back toward him. "Shit!" Longhorn steers could be controlled only when they wanted to be, and at the moment, these Longhorns had erupted into mass hysteria. He knew he needed to ride the other way, but he had to get Shannon. Her horse galloped dangerously close along the outside of the herd. As it was, he could barely see her red hair above all the dust, and he was pretty sure she'd lost her reins.

Luke grabbed his Winchester from the saddle and shot twice into the air. Thank goodness, the herd split and became a churning, milling mass. He was gripped by fear that Shannon would be trampled to death.

As if God knew Luke needed help, the sky opened up and rain became a deluge, pouring down on man, beast, and land. At least, it seemed to have calmed the herd, and he was able to make his way through the bawling, pushing animals.

Finally, Luke spotted Shannon on the ground. A tiny

speck, huddled in the middle of the cattle with her arms protecting her head.

"Get!" Luke waved his rope, and the cows scattered just like the sea parting, allowing him to reach Shannon. She looked up at him with sparkling green eyes, and his heart lodged in his throat. "Can you grab my hand?"

She managed to push herself to her feet, but then stumbled. He could see she was hurt as she limped toward him. He reached down and pulled her onto his horse, then wrapped his arms protectively around her. Luke wasted no time as he rode away from the herd. "Are you all right?"

"M--my foot."

"I'll look at it when we get back to the ranch. We don't want to stop here. This rain appears to be a real gully washer." He clicked his tongue and kneed his horse. "We'd best get home before another bolt of lightning sets the herd off again."

Shannon nodded. He tucked her head under his chin and nudged his horse into a gallop. As they rode, he kept thanking his lucky stars Shannon hadn't been killed. He felt like shaking her for the scare she'd given him, but at the same time he just wanted to hold her close. She trembled in his arms and his heart twisted.

It was then he realized Shannon McKinley was much more than a nanny to him.

---

12

*L*uke barged in through the back door carrying Shannon in his arms. He deposited her carefully in the nearest kitchen chair.

"Maria, find something so we can dry off," Luke ordered as he stepped back.

Shannon realized she was soaked and bruised as she took the towel from Maria and started drying her face and hair. She was damned lucky to be alive. If Luke hadn't found her in the midst of the cattle, she could have been trampled to death by the cattle.

"I was worried when I saw the sky so dark," Maria commented. "You should get out of your wet clothes, Señorita Shannon."

"I quite agree," Shannon said and tried to stand. "Oooo!" The pain in her foot shot straight up her leg, reminding her she wasn't going anywhere on her own.

"Sit down," Luke said in a harsh voice. "You shouldn't be standing," he added as if he realized his voice had sounded sharp. He bent down and took her boot in his palm and loosened the laces, carefully slipping it off her foot.

"Just what I figured, your ankle is swollen. You're not going to be able to put weight on it for awhile. I'm not a doctor but it could be broken."

Shannon was more aware of Luke's hands than her aching foot. "How am I goin' tae get aboot?"

Luke straightened and then rubbed his chin. "For now, I'll carry you to your room and Maria can help you change into some dry clothes. I need to get some dry duds on myself," he said as he bent over and scooped Shannon up.

"Ye canna carry me around forever."

"I agree. You're pretty heavy."

Shannon shoved him with her hand and Luke chuckled, but managed to add, "That was a fool thing riding out with a storm approaching."

She gave a rueful smile. "I think I've figured that out for myself."

"Storms pass quickly out here. As you can probably hear, it has already grown quiet." He turned the corner. "After we change into some dry clothing, we will take the buckboard to town so Doc Lindsey can look you over and see if something needs to be fixed."

Once they reached Shannon's room, Luke placed her on a chair. She smiled her thanks before he left her with Maria.

Maria assisted Shannon with her wet clothing, which felt as though they were glued to her skin. She had to stand on one foot and support herself with the chair. She felt pretty foolish needing someone's help getting her clothes off and on. She hadn't had a personal maid since England and had gotten used to being self-sufficient. However the English clothing was a little more complicated. Shannon slipped a blouse over her head. The warm dry clothes felt so much better than the wet ones.

"Can you help me with my hair, Maria?" Shannon asked.

"*Sí*." Maria took a fresh towel and dried Shannon's hair until most of the water was out. "I will plait your hair in a long braid since it is still wet."

"Thanks. Hopefully the doctor can do somethin' wit' my foot. The children dinna need tae see me helpless."

Maria laughed. "*Sí*, I can see them taking advantage of the situation."

"I dinna want tae think aboot being helpless." Shannon laughed.

THE AIR HAD TURNED MUCH COLDER by the time Luke carried Shannon out to the buckboard. "My goodness the weather changes quickly here," she commented.

"Probably the reason for the thunder and lightning. When the warm air and the cold air collide, it isn't good." Luke climbed up to his seat. He reached under the bench and pull out a red and yellow patchwork quilt, then handed it to her. "Here. This will help keep you warm."

"Back home," Shannon said as they pulled away from the ranch, "we heat bricks then place them under our feet when we travel."

"Strange," Luke said, then added, "But I bet it would work."

"Quite nicely."

They were quiet most the way until Luke finally broke the silence. Luke felt Shannon's leg next to his and he was surprised at how the slightest contact with this woman brought on the strongest urge to kiss her. However she seemed oblivious to the effect she had on him as she gazed out across the prairie like he wasn't there. "How's your foot?"

"It hurts. Especially when ye hit a bump."

Luke chuckled.

She glared. "'Tis not funny."

"I'm sorry. I'm sure it does hurt. I'll try and go around the ones up ahead. Maybe if you double the quilt it will give you a little more padding."

Shannon decided to take his advice and folded the quilt around her foot. "'Tis better. Thanks. Ye're bein' vera nice."

"I'm always nice."

"I beg to differ."

Luke took a deep breath and let it out slowly. He wanted her to understand. "I do care for you, Shannon," Luke admitted, then realized how true his words were. She was like a beacon of light that somehow brought a soft glow into his life. He couldn't stop himself from wanting her. "When I saw you disappear in that herd . . . I--I thought I'd lost you."

Shannon felt a strange restless craving by his softly spoken words. She was touched by Luke's concern and also uncertain about this change in him. "I thought I was gone, too, especially when the reins slipped from my grasp."

"We were lucky," Luke said. His left arm was propped on his knee, relaxing now that they were on their way. "However, I'd like to finish the conversation we'd started earlier. I still think we should marry."

"But --"

"Let me finish." He stopped her with a glance. "You need protection. Your father cannot force you to marry if you are already married."

"But ye dinna love me," she said in a small voice.

Luke sighed. He's forgotten how to be romantic. "Shannon, you have to realize my heart has been shut down for a very long time. I guess you could say that I've been dead inside," he admitted. "I like you. The children like you. Isn't that enough for now?"

She thought for a moment. This is what she wanted ... to marry Luke . . . her cowboy. So why was she suddenly reluctant? Deep down, she supposed she wanted to be swept off her feet and to feel loved and cherished. But that wasn't about to happen in this unsettled land.

Perhaps, if she went ahead and married Luke the rest would come later. "Ye said ye liked me?"

"Very much."

But deep down, she knew she'd never be happy until he loved her. "Then I guess it is for now."

"Good," Luke said as they approached the outskirts of Cottonwood. He pulled the team up in front of a brown building two doors down from the dry goods store. "Besides, I've missed the stage again."

Shannon laughed. "'Tis as good an excuse as any."

Luke carried her into Doc Lindsey's office and placed her on the examining table since no one was waiting in the outer room.

"What do we have here?" Doc Lindsey said as he shuffled over to the examining table. He was a portly man dressed in a worn, brown vest with the last two buttons open at the bottom. He appeared kind with a nice smile, Shannon thought.

"Hi Doc," Luke said and shook the man's hand. "This is Shannon McKinley, my children's nanny. Afraid she got caught in a stampede."

"What! It's a wonder she wasn't killed," Doc commented, his shock showing as his gray, bushy eyebrows snapped together. "Where did they step on you?"

"I was lucky. "'Tis just my foot." Shannon pointed.

"Let me see." Doc Lindsey sat on a nearby stool. He gently took her foot in his strong hands, moving it this way and that way.

Shannon groaned. It hurt like the dickens, but she didn't want to be a baby about something so minor. Hadn't she promised Luke she wouldn't get sick on him. Of course, she really wasn't sick, just a wee bit of a setback. She also noticed that Luke had slipped out of the room, and she wondered where he had gone.

"It doesn't appear that you've broken anything, but I expect it's going to be a couple of weeks before you can walk normally. I think it's just badly bruised and not sprained so you were very lucky." The doctor stood and rubbed his chin. "I tell you what, I'll bandage your foot, and then I've got a set of crutches in the back I can loan you, which will make it much easier to get around." His gaze fell on the bruise marring her cheekbone. "What about your head?"

Shannon laughed. "That was another accident. A long story, I'm afraid."

"Little lady, you need to take better care of yourself," he said, pushing the stool to the side. Then he went to the backroom.

It was just a moment before Doc Lindsey was back with the crutches, which were no more than long sticks with makeshift pads on the ends. She slipped gingerly off the table making sure to land on her good foot; she balanced herself with a hand on the table. The doctor placed each crutch under her arms, then helped her stand.

"How's that?"

"Not tae bad," Shannon said. "I think it wull take some getting used tae. Is there anythin' I can do for the pain?"

Doc Lindsey nodded then fetched a little brown bottle which he showed her before removing the cap. "This is laudanum." He gave her a spoonful. "Take a teaspoon before going to bed and it will help you sleep. You can take some in the daytime if you're in a lot of pain, but try to make do without. It can become habit forming."

"Thank ye," Shannon said while she hobbled out into the waiting room, wondering where Luke had gotten to.

She didn't have to wonder long because he swept into the office with a big smile which automatically made her suspicious. When did Luke ever smile?

"How is she, Doc?" Luke asked.

"She'll live. Lucky gal, nothing broken," Doc reported then filled Luke in on what Shannon should and shouldn't do. Luke paid the doctor, then slipped the bottle of laudanum in his pocket.

He held open the door for Shannon so she could move through it easily. When she started for the wagon, Luke caught her arm. "Not so fast. We need to go and see the Miller sisters."

Shannon was too startled by his suggestion to offer any objection. "I dinna think ye like them."

He helped Shannon along the boardwalk. "I have to amit they take some getting used to, but I knew they would want to witness our wedding."

She stopped. "What?"

"Didn't we discuss getting married on the way into town?"

Shannon was totally bewildered at Luke's behavior. "Aye. But I dinna think it would be today!"

Luke shrugged matter-of-factly. "No time like the present."

Shannon knew she should feel some semblance of happiness. Her mind refused to register the significance of his words. Luke was really going to marry her and not send her back on the stage, but actually marry her. "What about the children?" she asked. How were they going to feel when Luke told them she was their new mother?

"Well." Luke frowned, realizing that he really hadn't thought of the children. "I'd like for them to be present. However, I'll be leaving once they come home tomorrow and there will not be much time. I want to get this out of the way."

Shannon gaped at him. "Ye are romantic. I'll give ye that."

Luke held the door open to the dry goods store, and she was glad that he did have the decency to look embarrassed. "I'll admit it isn't the best way, but I'll make it up to you, I promise."

Shannon started to tell him he didn't owe her anything, but she realized this was a big step for Luke. She knew that she already loved Luke and his children, and wasn't this one step closer to having the family she'd always wanted? Shannon just hoped that Luke would one day love her.

"Here they are." Thelma swept to the front of the store to greet them. She clapped her hands together. "We're so happy you're gettin' married."

"How did ye know?" Shannon asked, puzzled when she'd just found out herself.

"Luke came by and told us while you were at the doctor's."

"'Tis kind o' sudden," Shannon murmured as she hugged Thelma.

"Nonsense." Emma joined them. "There's no time like the present and it's about time that Luke came to his senses."

Luke frowned, a shadow of annoyance crossing his face. "Thank you, ladies, for you vote of confidence."

"If we didn't think you were right for each other," Emma

said, pausing until Luke turned back around. "We'd tell her to run."

Shannon started laughing. Luke shook his head. He made his way to the back of the store where a short man in a brown suit stood. She assumed he was the preacher since he clutched a bible in his hand.

Thelma took Shannon by the arm, gaining her attention. "Let's get you changed."

"I beg yer pardon," Shannon said as she hobbled to the back.

"You might not be having a fancy wedding but, at least, you'll have a wedding dress," Emma said. "It's the least we can do."

"Ye huv such a dress?"

"Come on in the back with us," Emma said as she opened the door behind the counter. "We'll be right back, gentlemen."

Shannon felt like she was in a fog, everything was happening so quickly. She adjusted her breathing once she realized she was breathing too fast and becoming light-headed. It wouldn't be good to pass out on the floor and have to turn around and head back to the doctor's office.

Thelma held out a white grown of satin and lace. "Here it is."

"Oh my." Shannon covered her mouth with her hand and one of the crutches crashed to the floor. "'Tis beautiful."

Emma stooped over and picked up the crutch. She propped it against the wall and then took the other one and did the same. "You're not going to need these for a few minutes, honey. And by the looks of these crutches, he needs to take better care of you." Emma clicked her tongue. "Now, let's get you dressed so you won't have an impatient groom."

"I'm not tae sure about him bein' impatient," Shannon murmured as she slipped out of her clothes. "He doesn't seem tae be too romantic."

"Nonsense," Emma scoffed. "Most men aren't. But we can see that he honestly cares about you. There is something in his eyes that makes him look like he's alive again. And believe me that's saying something because he has had that dead look for a long, long time. I think you're going to be real good for him, honey."

"I hope yer right," Shannon said. She turned around with a hop. "How do I look?"

Thelma clapped her hands together. "Beautiful, child. This was my wedding gown once upon a time. When I was much smaller." She smiled then added, "And younger. Here, let's get you back on those crutches. Don't want you falling down."

Shannon limped from the back room over to where Luke stood. Despite the crutches, Luke couldn't believe how beautiful she looked in a vision of white satin, and he said so, "You look lovely."

"The crutches dinna help." Shannon smiled as she joined him. They faced the preacher, then Luke whispered, "I barely noticed."

Something in Shannon's stomach fluttered.

The ceremony was short and the only part Shannon remembered was when the preacher said Luke could kiss the bride. What started out as a simple kiss engulfed into flame of passion once she slipped her arms around his neck. The crutches fell to the floor with a bang and were forgotten. They only broke apart when the preacher cleared his throat... twice.

Flustered, Shannon pulled back. She hoped the kiss affected Luke as much as it had her. No one could kiss like that and feel nothing so Luke must feel something for her. Finally, she turned to shake the preacher's hand and then Thelma and Emma's.

Shannon changed back into her own clothes even when Thelma insisted she wear the gown home. "I canna risk something happening tae yer gown." She'd never forgive herself.

After that, Shannon didn't remember anything until they had reached the ranch. The medicine had made her numb, but at least her foot didn't throb anymore.

ONCE THEY WERE BACK at the ranch, Luke cleared his throat to gain her attention. "It's late. Why don't you get what you need for tonight?" He sounded so business-like that she frowned. "Tomorrow Maria can move your things into my room." He climbed down off the wagon and came around to her side. "I'm going to take the wagon to the barn. We can tell Maria and everyone our news in the morning. The children should be home by then."

Shannon managed to nod.

He reached up and helped her down then grabbed the crutches out of the back of the wagon. "Are you all right?" Luke asked. "I don't ever remember you being this quiet."

"Aye. 'Tis just . . . ye huv tae admit it has been a vera busy day. I kindna feel like I'm dreamin', and I'm waitin' for someone tae wake me up."

Luke smiled at her. "I feel the same. A lot has happened today, but I guarantee you're not dreaming. Run along and get your things, and I'll be in shortly." He looked like he wanted to swat her on the backside as he would a cow to get her moving along. She was glad he didn't . . . he'd probably knock her off her crutches.

Shannon frowned at his words, but she knew what he meant. Or did she? Was he anxious to get her into his bed? She'd been rushed all day, and she was sleepy from the medicine, which she thought could be making her irritable. Instead of saying something she might regret later, she simply nodded and stumbled into the house, thankful that everyone was in bed.

Once she had moved a few things to Luke's room, she changed her clothes, wanting to be finished before Luke came back. It had been difficult, tucking things under her arms and chin to get them moved. Now she was nervous and unsure what to expect. She yawned. Would he want to make love to her? It was their honeymoon. She wasn't sure what she should do so she hobbled over to bed and, being very careful of her bandaged foot, climbed under the covers. She definitely didn't feel desirable with crutches under her arms.

When Luke entered the room, he smiled. "I see it didn't take you long to slip into bed." He kicked off his boots, then stripped quickly out of his clothes before he turned off the lamp next to the bed.

Luke crawled under the covers, reached over and pulled Shannon close to him. "You don't have to be so tense," he murmured. "I know we're still practically strangers . . . well except for last night." He paused and swallowed hard. "I've been thinking. I'd like to take things slow between us. We'll not make love tonight, partly because I don't want to kick your foot and further injure it."

And the other part, Shannon wondered, not sure if she was disappointed or relieved over his concern for her injury. Nevertheless, she took a deep breath and relaxed. "I think 'tis a good idea. It has been a verra long day." She yawned again. "Sorry. I want ye tae know I will make ye a good wife."

"I don't doubt that, Shannon." He placed a light kiss on her forehead. "Let's get some sleep. Tomorrow will be here before you know it."

------

13

*S*hannon awoke with a jerk. It took her a moment to remember why she was in Luke's bed. The laudanum from the night before made her head feel fuzzy. She frowned. When she should be absolutely happy that she'd married the man she loved, she felt unsure of herself.

Every muscle in her body ached this morning as she struggled to sit up in bed. In doing so, she bumped her foot and yesterday's events rushed back to her.

No wonder she was sore. She felt as if the cattle had run over her instead of around her and her foot throbbed. She really didn't feel like a bride, but sitting here in bed with her troubled thoughts would get her nowhere.

A knock on the door caught her attention. "Come in," she called.

Maria swept into the room with a robe thrown over her arm and a bright smile. "Congratulations! Señior Luke told me you were married yesterday." She smiled and gave a nod of approval. "I'm so happy for you, *sí*. Now the *niños* will have a mother again."

"Thanks. I'm so happy ye approve," Shannon murmured

as she held her hand out for the robe. "I think I'm going tae need some help, Maria. I'm very sore from my little adventure yesterday." Shannon groaned as she swung her legs off the bed. "I huv muscles that I dinna know I had."

"*Sí*, I thought as much. You're very lucky the cattle didn't trample you," Maria said as she helped Shannon stand. Maria grabbed the crutches propped against the wall and handed them to Shannon. "I prepared a warm bath. I hope it will help with your soreness."

"Oh, thank ye," Shannon said gratefully as she hobbled behind Maria to the bathing room. Once she'd removed her bandage from her black and blue foot she sank into the warm water. "Oh my, 'tis heaven," she sighed, then she glanced up at Maria. "Do ye huv a hand mirror?"

"*Sí*." Maria turned and walked over to a brown dresser where she retrieved a small oval mirror and handed it to Shannon.

"Oh my! 'Tis something," Shannon commented as she took in her appearance. The lump on her forehead had gone down some but there was a bruise on the side of her head where she'd been hit, and a couple of scratches on her cheek. "I wasn't a verra pretty bride."

"Oh, no, señorita. I don't think Señor Luke was thinking about that.. He seemed so worried. He has not acted that way since his wife was sick." Maria placed a couple of towels close to the tub, then continued, "I believe he cares for you very much, señorita." She blushed at her boldness.

"Thank ye fer saying so, Maria." Shannon lathered her arms with the bar of soap then rinsed them off. "Everythin' has been so sudden I'm not sure how I feel. If ye will help me wash my hair, I might feel more like a woman."

Later, as Maria dried Shannon's hair, she said, "The

niños, they will be back today. They will be surprised they have a new mother."

"I hope they wull be happy," Shannon said, but she had her doubts.

SOMETIME AROUND NOON Travis and the children returned home. Luke called for Shannon to join him and together they went outside to greet everyone.

The wagon lumbered to a stop and then Travis who had been riding behind the wagon trotted up to where they stood. Instantly, his smile faded.

"What the hell happened to her?"

"I married her," Luke replied.

"What!" Travis shouted and rolled his eyes heavenward. "Did you have to beat her first so she would say yes?"

Shannon laughed. "I can see where ye might think that."

Luke smiled, too. "Shannon was caught in the middle of a stampede and lived to tell of it."

"I've only been gone a couple of days and everything seems to have happened while I was gone." Travis shook his head as he dismounted. "How the hell did she get in the middle of a bunch of cows?"

"Long story," Luke said.

The children who were stepping down from the wagon hadn't paid any attention to the grownups as they had been asleep and only woke up once the wagon had stopped.

Toby was the first to reach his father. "Did you miss us, Pa?" He didn't give his father a chance to answer as he hugged Luke's leg.

"Yes, I did," Luke said. He reached down and ruffled Toby's hair. "How was your visit with your aunt and uncle?"

Molly shuffled over and hugged her father, too. "Aunt Ann is going to have the baby very soon. She's huge." Molly held her arms in a big circle in front of her stomach.

"I bet she is."

"Miss Shannon, why are you propped up on sticks?" Toby asked.

"I had a small accident, Toby, and bruised my foot. I must use these," she shook a crutch, "for a few days tae help me walk."

Toby scrunched his nose up looking very serious. "You're going to have a hard time playing hopscotch with me."

"Aye, but ye can practice until I'm well again."

"I have some good news for you two," Luke said, sliding closer to Shannon.

"What Pa?" Toby asked.

Luke slipped his arm around Shannon. "While you were gone Miss Shannon and I got married. You now have a new mother."

It was as if time stood still, Shannon thought. Molly hadn't even said hello, and she appeared very unhappy. Toby looked confused. His mouth had fallen opened.

"I don't want a mother!" Molly screamed and ran toward the house.

"Does that mean no more school work?" Toby asked.

"Afraid not," Shannon said with a smile. "We wull continue with the lessons same as before. Remember ye want tae be smart like yer father."

Toby thought for a moment. "Do I have to call you ma?"

"Ye can call me whatever ye want and feel comfortable with."

"Fine," Toby said with a shrug. "I'm hungry." He turned and ran toward the house.

"You'd think that they get a mother every day," Shannon

mumbled. A wee bit of her had hoped they would be happy, but that was probably too much to hope for this soon. Change was always hard. She knew that firsthand. So she'd work with the children and hope they would learn to love her.

"It'll take some adjustment," Luke said with a sigh, but he gave her waist a reassuring squeeze. "They will come around. I'll go speak to Molly."

After Luke had gone to the house, Travis strolled over to stand in front of her. "Well, I'll tell you." He pulled her to him in a big hug, knocking the crutch from beneath her arm, "Welcome to the family. This group has needed someone ever since Ruth died."

Shannon tilted her chin up to look at Travis. She smiled her appreciation. "Thanks. I believe we all wull huv some adjusting tae do."

"Luke is right. The kids will come around. They didn't like the fact you had been hurt back in town." Travis released her, then stooped to pick up her crutches. "Luke and the children need you."

"I'm not tae sure."

"Trust me." Travis reached out and squeezed her arm. "My brother has been a shell of a man since his wife died. He'll always blame himself for her death."

"Why?"

"Ruth wasn't crazy about living in Texas, but Luke promised to build her a big house. They were happy but Ruth tended to get sick often, and then one time she came down with a raging fever they couldn't control. Believe me, Luke and the doctor tried everything, but in the end Ruth was too weak to fight. My brother always blamed himself."

"So sad," Shannon said.

Travis shook his head, "When I first arrived, I could

tell right away that Luke had changed. He had a light in his eyes once again." Travis smiled. "And you're the reason."

Shannon shrugged. Had she made a difference in Luke? She would like to think so. Her thoughts filtered back to the day she'd met him. He definitely wasn't happy then. So maybe they had made progress since she wasn't on a coach heading back to New Orleans. She smiled, feeling a little better.

～

LUKE FOUND Molly face down on the bed crying. Her dirty blond hair spread over her arms, hiding the child's face, but the sniffles could be heard. He entered her room and closed the door behind him.

After easing down on the side of the bed, he placed his right hand on Molly's back. "Why are you crying?" Luke asked softly.

She raised a tear-streaked face to him. "I--I don't want *her* for a mother."

"Why?"

"Because."

Luke reached over and took her small hand in his. "That really isn't much of a reason. Do you think Shannon will replace your mother?"

Molly nodded.

"I thought so, but no one can ever replace your mother. She was a very special woman, and I knew her a lot longer than you did." He squeezed Molly's hand. "Your mother would be disappointed in the way you are acting."

Molly wiggled her hand from his, then sat up straighter and rubbed her eyes. "She would? Why?"

"Because she would want someone else to come into your life to show you how to be a lady."

"I don't wanna to be no lady."

"You will one day, and there are certain things that I can't do for you that Shannon can," he paused. "Besides, I thought you liked her?"

"She's all right."

"Well, now you won't have any more nannies, so there won't be any changes in your life from now on, and we'll be a family again."

When he didn't receive any comment, Luke continued, "I'm going to have to go away for a few days with Uncle Travis. I want you to behave while I'm gone. Shannon has been hurt and needs your help.

Molly threw her arms around his neck. "I don't want you to go, Pa."

"I don't want to go either, sweetheart, but it's necessary to keep everyone safe. I'll be back before you know it."

LATER THAT NIGHT when Shannon and Luke were alone, they lay in bed talking, a candle burned low beside the bed.

"I hate I'll have to leave you so soon, but I feel it's something I have to do. We cannot stay under Mexico's rule much longer," Luke said. He slipped his arm around her and pulled her next to him.

Shannon's hand rested flat on Luke's chest. This felt so comfortable and right, she thought. She tilted her head back so she could look up at his strong face. "'Tis necessary. Back home we felt the same aboot the English. They were always tellin' us what we could and couldn't do. Ye needn't be worryin', we'll be here when ye return."

She moved slightly so she could see Luke. She couldn't quit staring at him, remembering how it felt when she'd kissed him. She felt a ripple of excitement. His brown hair was slicked back away from his hard features, and his eyes appeared like embers in the candlelight. The smoldering flame she saw in his gaze startled her, and for once he wasn't hiding his feelings. She was filled with a strange inner-excitement because his nearness made her senses spin.

She laid her head back on his chest, her fingers making small circles on his chest. Luke was so big and strong and disturbing in every way. She was well aware of the muscles beneath her fingertips. A profound longing to reach over and taste his lips consumed her. But all this was new to her. She wanted Luke to make the first move to show that he really cared for her.

Luke watched the way Shannon's hair floated around her shoulders. The soft flesh beneath his hands promised the woman he held was indeed his wife. How many years had he been without the company of a woman? He could feel an invisible web of attraction building between them, so powerful that his skin tingled.

He tilted her chin so he could see her face more clearly. Was that desire he saw flash in her eyes? The knowledge that she experienced the same feelings that he did, felt like a prairie fire sweeping over him, causing him to harden and throb. He couldn't stop himself from rubbing his thumb back and forth across her lips. She was drawing him to her just like a thirsty animal to water.

He bent his head, his mouth mere inches from hers. "I want to make love to you Shannon," Luke whispered. "Is your foot too sore? I don't want to hurt you."

"Dinna worry aboot my foot, Luke Griffin. I want ye, too," she murmured as her arms snaked around his neck.

The small gesture and her admission pushed Luke completely over the edge. Somewhere in the back of his mind, he remembered he'd said something about going slow. Slow was the furthest thing from his mind. He pulled Shannon up to him, their naked bodies fitting perfectly as he kissed the side of her neck. Hot skin next to hot skin.

"You really don't know what you're doing to me," he murmured as he trailed kisses up her chin.

He felt Shannon tremble as he tenderly kissed her earlobe. Her back was smooth. Her skin silky. He'd never felt anything so soft . . . so inviting. Her breast crushed next to his chest were much too tempting, he thought as his lips sought hers. The sweetness of Shannon's mouth caused him to groan. His tongue stroked and caressed hers until Shannon responded with a passion of her own, feeding his hunger. "You make me forget everything."

She looked at him and whispered, "Ye are the bravest mon I've ever met, Luke Griffin." She nibbled the side of his mouth as she added. "Ye now have a family that loves ye verra much."

Her words would remain in Luke's mind forever, as would her scent. It seemed to fill his soul. Luke finally felt that he was beginning a new life, and he could put the past behind him.

Shannon desperately wanted to learn how to please Luke. When she touched her tongue to his, instinct told her she was doing something right because she felt him shiver slightly. As her tongue tangled with his, Luke's hand slid up the side of her breast, covering it possessively. He outlined the tip of her breast with his finger.

His mouth left hers. Ever so slowly, he lowered his head where his lips touched her nipple with tantalizing possessiveness. He fastened his mouth to her breast and began to suckle. A sudden heat swept over her and she moaned with pleasure. Embarrassed by her action, she had no time to dwell on the matter. His mouth vacated her breast. And then his tongue licked a hot path across her skin where his lips fastened around her other breast as his tongue teased her nipple. She was barely aware that his hand had moved lower until he touched her thigh, causing her to jump.

"There shouldn't be any pain this time," Luke soothed. "It is only the first time that there is pain."

"Are ye sure?"

"I'm sure," Luke said.

She relaxed and opened her legs for him. His fingers slid between her curls and began to massage her. Shannon arched against his hand. She tried to look into Luke's eyes but he was trailing kisses down her stomach until his lips replaced his fingers and a jolt of pleasure shot through her, much stronger than before. She began to whimper for something . . . she wasn't sure what. He was right this was different from the first time they had made love. She couldn't help whispering his name, "Luke."

When she thought she could take no more, Luke recaptured her lips in a kiss like none before. His lips were demanding, and she tried to give back all she could.

Luke had never known lovemaking could be this good. And it was taking every ounce of strength to hold back. He cursed himself for wanting her. But when she whispered his name, he was hurtled beyond a point of no return. Then he remembered Shannon was now his wife. Warmth of a different nature spread through him; marrying her had been the best thing he'd done in a long while.

He positioned himself to enter her with a strong thrust only then did he feel her tightness just as she gasped. "Did I hurt you?"

"Nay. 'Twas just a surprise."

Luke waited until her body had adjusted, but the heat filling his loins was so unbearable he needed to move again . . . slower . . . steady until Shannon began to move with him. She wrapped her legs around him and arched her hips so he could move freely. He'd found heaven.

Shannon had lost complete control. Never feeling like this before, she marveled at the completeness she felt as Luke plunged one final time and shuddered at the same time she saw white lights exploding all around her. She savored the feeling of satisfaction, the shortness of breath and the happiness swelling within her.

Luke collapsed against her, then rolled to the side, still keeping her within his arms, "We're now officially married Mrs. Griffin," he said huskily.

She heard his hard breathing as she rubbed her hands up and down his back. "I like the sound of that, Mr. Griffin, and I like it when ye hold me this way."

"I like it, too," Luke admitted before he drifted off into a very peaceful sleep.

14

The sun peeked over the horizon as Luke and Travis rode out early before the rest of the household had begun to stir. Luke thought it would be easier on the children if there weren't any tearful goodbyes. Besides, he wasn't sure how long he would be gone and didn't want to lie when they posed the question.

Just as they rode up the small hill behind the ranch, Luke thought he saw something in the clump of trees that was a few yards away. He twisted in the saddle to get a better view.

"What's wrong?" Travis asked.

"Nothing. Thought I saw something. Guess I'm not fully awake since I'm jumping at shadows this morning."

"I appreciate you leaving the children for this one mission," Travis said. "Austin said he wants to take San Antonio, but some other towns need to be taken before he gets there."

"Have you actually joined the army?"

"Didn't have to. They're using both enlisted men and

volunteers. We—" Travis pointed to his chest. "--Are the volunteers."

"Are you going on to San Antonio afterwards?

"Nope. I've been asked to join a 'Corps of Rangers.'"

Luke frowned. "Haven't heard of them."

"Not surprised," Travis replied. "They're trying to get a group of men ... I guess you could call them lawmen who will protect against outlaws and Indians."

"Sounds like a good job for you. You never have liked staying in one place long."

"We've got a motto," Travis said with a smile. "Ride like a Mexican . . . Trail like a Tennessean . . . And fight like the devil."

Luke chuckled. "That's in the future. Let's talk about the present. How many men do the Mexicans have?"

"Seven hundred fifty last count."

Luke rubbed his chin. "Hmm, not sure I like those numbers. We're still out numbered."

"True." Travis nodded. "But smarter."

Luke laughed, feeling some of the tension ease from his neck. "Has it occurred to you the Mexicans are probably saying the same thing?"

"Probably," Travis admitted as he shifted in the saddle. "We'll have that to consider when we get there. We have a good group of men so I'm not worried. Changing the subject, I'm glad you got married."

"Thanks."

They rode around a ravine before straightening so they could ride side by side.

"I think Shannon is a good choice and someone who can handle your children," Travis said, but added, "As we know they can be a handful."

"I know." Luke sighed. "It's my fault. I let them run wild

after their mother died." He slowed his horse to a trot since they had been moving at a good pace for a couple of hours. "I kind of hate leaving Shannon on crutches. Let's hope she's still there when we return."

"You know it's bad when you have to marry the nanny to keep her." Travis smiled.

"Oh, shut up," Luke snapped. "You do know one of these days you're bound to get married, settle down, and then I'm going to rib you to no end." Luke wasn't going to put up with his brother needling him. "By the way, where are we going?"

"Gonzales. Maybe Mission Concepción," Travis replied. He pointed. "See that rider up yonder under the oak tree?"

Luke peered up ahead and sure enough there was someone mounted on his horse sitting under a tree. He appeared to be waiting for them. "Yep."

"It's Deaf Smith. He'll tell us where we're needed."

"Who?"

"Erastus Smith. He's kind of hard of hearing so remember to speak loud. He'll ride with us the rest of the way."

"Are the rest of the men afflicted?" Luke asked with an arched brow, imagining the ragtag army he'd yet to meet ... one couldn't hear . . . one couldn't see . . . another couldn't walk. *Yep, this battle would be a cinch.*

"Nope. Believe it or not Deaf Smith is the best damn tracker around," Travis told him as they slowed their mounts.

"Howdy folks," Deaf said with a slow drawl. "You ready to ride?" A medium built man with a high forehead and a copious nose, Deaf's brick-colored hair gave him a warm, friendly appearance.

"Deaf." Travis motioned toward Luke. "This is my brother, Luke."

"Nice to meet you." Deaf gave a quick nod. "Let's get the lead out. Don't want to get caught by the Mexicans. There's a water hole up ahead. We can stop there, water the horses, then I'll answer your questions."

They rode at a good clip each man lost in his own thoughts. The land was flat and they could make good time. The sun had broken through the clouds, taking away the morning chill.

Finally a small stream came into view, and they halted the horses to give them a rest and to get water.

Travis dismounted. "We still going to Gonzales?"

"Nope," Deaf said, then spit out a stream of tobacco juice. "We took that one with eighteen men."

"No shit," Travis said.

Luke added, "Impressive."

"Yep. Didn't believe it myself. Got that gol-dang old cannon back, too," Deaf said with a twinkle in his eye. "And you know it's the damnedest thing. They stitched a wedding dress into a flag bearing a black cannon and the words 'Come and take it', then hung it on the front of the cannon so everyone could see."

"Did we have any cannonballs?" Travis asked.

"Nope. Shot pieces of scrap metal," Deaf said with a laugh. "Heard tell that they're callin' it the first shot of the Texas Revolution."

"Any casualties?" Luke asked Deaf.

"Nope not a one."

Luke nodded and said, "Let's hope our luck continues, so it'll be a short war."

Mounting once again, the three men rode through hills dotted with mesquite trees and scrub brush. They had only ridden about an hour when Luke spoke up again, "Well, I'll be damned if it isn't George."

Up ahead standing next to his horse was their third brother, George. George's head snapped up as the group approached.

"Well, look what the dogs dragged up," George said with a smile. He was the oldest of the three, and shorter by a head than the other two.

Luke and Travis dismounted and gave their brother a hug.

"Damn, it's good to see you," Luke said. "It's been too long."

"Glad you could join us," Travis chimed in, and then turned to Deaf. "Deaf, this is our older brother George. I told him what we were going to do, but never expected him to show up."

"Damn glad you did, boy. We need as many as we can get." Deaf leaned down and shook George's hand. "Looks like the Griffin boys are well represented. Any more of ya?"

"Just the three of us." Luke removed his hat and slapped it on his leg to remove the dust. "It's been a long haul since the three of us have been together. Ashamed it has to be in a battle."

"Like I said, it's good to have you, however, you three need to quit jaw-jacking and let's ride before the next skirmish starts without us," Deaf told them. "Ya'll can catch up tonight when we camp. Let's ride."

Hefting himself back into the saddle, Luke snatched up the reins and followed after the others, his thought churning at something Deaf had said earlier. According to Deaf they should reach the mission late tomorrow. And Luke found he was anxious to get this over with and return home. A small fact that really surprised him. He missed Shannon.

~

TRUE TO DEAF'S WORD, it was nearing dusk when they arrived at the Mission Concepción. The whitewashed walls of the mission seemed to have risen up from the brown dirt that surrounded it. However they didn't stop at the mission but rode a little ways to what appeared to be a group of men already gathered. Deaf had told them while they were riding that Jim Bowie would be leading this attack.

There he was up ahead. "Gentleman. Glad you could join us. I'm Jim Bowie. Our other division will be commanded by Fannin." Bowie nodded toward them and immediately turned to Deaf. "Deaf, you need to go and scout the Mexicans, so we know what we're up against. Grab a fresh horse then head on out."

Luke had heard stories of Jim Bowie, but had never met him. The man was famous for his famed "Bowie Knife" – it was a one-edged blade that was so perfectly balanced it could be thrown twenty feet and kill a man on the spot.

Bowie was an Indian-fighter who hailed from Tennessee. Yet here he was helping the Texas cause. Maybe the man just enjoyed fighting and that was what brought him to Texas. No matter the reason, Luke was glad to have an experienced leader.

After Deaf had ridden off, Bowie turned to the others. "Welcome to Mission Concepción. We arrived yesterday and set up in that horseshoe-shaped gully over there. We will be on one end and Fannin's men on the other." He pointed. "Go ahead and get yourself a good position. We'll know more when Deaf reports back." Bowie rubbed the back of his neck. "Doubt that anything will happen before morning, so relax while you can. Let me know if you need anything."

The three of them rode toward the dried river bottom,

which was located about five hundred yards from the mission. The riverbed was skirted with timber. They spotted the edge and peered in the long gully, which was a hundred yards wide. This would be perfect. A naturally strong position with the flat plain extended before them.

They followed the rim until they found an opening where they could ride their mounts down to the riverbed. They rode along nodding to the groups of men scattered along the wall until they found a good place. It was time to settled down for the night. They tied their horses and rubbed them down before making their own camp.

Callum grew impatient.

He sat with his back to a bolder eating a plate of eggs he had stolen from the henhouse. What he would give to have some meat and ale.

At least he'd had some company when Alasdair had been with him, but now it was sit and wait. He was sick of this shit. He'd give it one more week, and if Shannon didn't ride out on her own, then he was going to drag her out of that house all the way back to Scotland.

He couldn't return to Scotland without the lass or the jewels. The lass would help bring honor back to the clan, and the jewels would bring wealth. And he would be back in his homeland and out of this dull brown country.

The next couple days were not pleasant.

The children had moped around once they found out their father had left without saying goodbye.

Shannon was a little surprised by how much she missed Luke. Things were not the same . . . the house felt empty, which was silly since it was full of children and servants. She wondered if Luke missed her. Had he thought about her? She hoped he did.

They both had changed in the short time they had been together. Luke's ruggedness still drew her in, but she'd like to think she had softened him a little. She knew he was a little more open than when she'd first met him, and she felt good things were ahead of them. She shook her head which seemed to be in the clouds this morning.

She still couldn't put her full weight on her ankle. With the crutch hurting under her arm, she'd been elated when she'd spotted a cane in the pantry off the kitchen. Using the smooth piece of wood to walk was more rewarding than the crutches. She still couldn't move quickly, but it felt much better. She was thankful that her foot had only been bruised. If it had been sprained or broken she would have required the crutches for a lot longer. As she hobbled down the hallway, she knew it was time to get back to a routine.

The children were settled at their desks when Shannon finally made it to the classroom.

"Good morning," Shannon said as she took the seat behind her desk. Molly's resentful glares told Shannon that the child was still upset.

Shannon placed the papers she'd had in her hand on her desk. She sorted the paperwork until she found the two sheets of paper she needed.

"Today we are goin' tae huv a short arithmetic test tae see how well ye remember what I've taught ye. Come and get yer test and then ye can began."

While they were busy, Shannon took out two readers

and turned them to the page where she wanted the children to begin.

Toby brought his paper up first. "Here," he said.

"Very good. Ye can read the first chapter of this book while I grade yer paper."

A few minutes later Molly tossed her paper on Shannon's desk but didn't bother to say anything. Shannon raised her brow but chose not to reprimand Molly this time. "Here is yer book."

"Yeah, I know, read the first chapter," Molly tried to snatch the book from her, but Shannon held tight.

"Are you going to give me the book?" Molly asked.

Shannon fought to rein in her temper. "Hold out your hand." When the child followed instructions, Shannon placed the book in her hand. "Now ye can read."

Molly frowned but didn't say anything.

After Shannon finished grading the papers, she grimaced. Molly had only gotten two problems correct.

"Molly, is there something ye dinna understand with yer figures? Ye were doing better a few weeks ago."

"Nope."

"You only had two problems that were correct."

"So."

"Yer brother only got three wrong, sae I'd say he is now smarter than his big sister."

"You're dumb, Molly," Toby piped up.

"'Tisn't nice tae call someone dumb, Toby," Shannon corrected.

"Well, it's true. You just said so."

"I don't need to know arithmetic," Molly informed both of them.

"I think ye do," Shannon said calmly. "Toby, ye can go and play while I work with Molly."

"Goodie." Toby jumped up. "Can I go outside?"

"As long as ye stay close tae the house. We'll be outside shortly."

Shannon patted the chair next to her. "Come and sit next tae me, Molly."

Molly rolled her eyes, but did as she was told.

Shannon took out the test and went over each problem, asking Molly to add the numbers. She seemed to know each answer, which told Shannon the child had failed the test on purpose.

"Molly ye ken that ye're not hurting anyone but yerself when ye dinna do ye best."

"I don't care!"

"Watch yer tone, young lady," Shannon snapped, then counted to ten before she continued, "Ye dinna want yer pa tae be proud of ye?"

"Sure I do. But I don't want a new mother."

Shannon sighed. "I'll never replace yer mother, Molly. She will always be yers. But I do hope we wull be friends one day."

Molly jumped up. "I don't need a friend." She darted from the classroom before Shannon could call her back.

Well, that most certainly hadn't gone well, Shannon thought. She got up and started putting away the children's books and papers. How was she going to get through to Molly? The problem was she knew how Molly felt about losing her mother. It was one of the hardest things a child could go through ... the loss ... the hurt of never seeing them again.

Maybe if she left Molly to herself, she'd finally come around and not be so resentful.

Shannon limped down the hall to the kitchen to fetch a cup of tea and to see a friendly face.

Maria smiled upon seeing her. "When I saw Molly come flying through the kitchen, I thought you might need some tea." Maria handed a steaming cup to Shannon.

"Bless ye," Shannon smiled. She took the cup of tea, then moved to the window where she could glance out and watch the children. "Motherhood is harder than I thought it would be."

"*Sí*, I think it's because Molly was so close to her mother. She used to follow her all around the house."

"I actually ken how she feels having lost my own mother. Perhaps one day she can let go of her anger, and then we can become friends."

"*Sí*, then again maybe it is a mother that Molly needs."

Shannon swung around knowing she had a completely dumfounded expression on her face because she had no idea what she needed to do.

"I'M GOING TO RUN AWAY," Molly told Toby as they played hopscotch beside the barn.

Toby picked up his stone. "Why?"

"'Cause if I run away . . . Pa will come home sooner. You heard *her* tell us she didn't know when he would be home. He'll be upset and send *her* away."

"I like Miss Shannon," Toby said. "Why don't you like her anymore?"

Molly threw her stone and it landed next to the top block. "Don't you see that she's taking Ma's place? Everything is changing."

"I don't think of her like Ma, but I still like her. My turn," Toby said as he positioned himself at the first block. "Miss Shannon is better than all those old nannies that we had, and she's made me much smarter than you." He grinned as he hopped back to the starting block.

"You stepped on a line. It's my turn." Molly shoved Toby out of the way. "You're too little. You don't understand." She tossed her stone and missed the top block completely. "This is a stupid game."

Toby laughed. "Only because I'm better at this, too."

"I'm just not paying attention."

"Sooo--" Toby hopped. "W--what are you going to do?"

"Tonight after we're supposed to go to bed, I'm going to slip out and run away."

"Where you gonna go?"

"Don't know. I'll get a horse and go and hide somewhere until Pa comes and finds me."

"Don't think you should do that, Molly."

"I don't care what you think," Molly told him, then grabbed Toby's shirtfront. "And you better not tell them until tomorrow morning. You hear me?"

15

*C*allum couldn't believe his luck.

He had just settled down for the night, thinking it had been another wasted day, when he heard a horse and rider coming his direction.

He jumped to his feet, then scrambled to hide behind a boulder while he waited for the right moment. The rider appeared small. Perhaps Shannon was coming his way. However, he doubted he could be so lucky. When the horse and rider moved into the tree line, Callum sprang and grabbed the horse's halter before the animal could bolt.

"Who are you?" A child squealed.

Callum jerked her from the horse before she could scream again. He recognized her as one of the children from the ranch. He'd seen Shannon playing with her.

Saints above. He didn't have time to calm down a squirming *bairn*. He snatched a piece of cloth and gagged the child, and then he tied her hands.

"Ye can quit yer crying. It won't do ye any good," he informed her as he sat her on the boulder.

Callum had to move quickly before someone came

looking for the bairn. He packed up his meager belongings and then glanced around to see if he had forgotten anything. There was just one more thing he needed to do.

He pulled a sheet of paper and a pencil out of his saddlebag. Quickly, Callum scribbled a note to Shannon as he thought, *this should get the lass out of the house where he could grab her.* He envisioned the green hills of Scotland and longed to be in his homeland once more.

He took the child's horse and tied the reins to a tree limb. Callum placed the note under the edge of the saddle where ranch hands would easily see it when they came looking for the child.

Callum mounted, then positioned the *bairn* in front of him. A slow smile slid across his face. "Aye," he said to himself. The lass would come for the child. He knew it.

SOMETHING WAS WRONG. Shannon couldn't quite put her finger on the strange feeling she had upon waking this morning. She had been breathing so fast it scared her. But now she couldn't remember the dream.

She retrieved her clothes off the back of the chair where Maria had left them, which made it easier for Shannon. She finished dressing in a simple brown skirt and white linen blouse. Pulling her hair back, she tied a pretty yellow ribbon around her ponytail.

Now that she was dressed, she once again had that odd feeling. Perhaps it was the dream she couldn't recall. She thought about it a moment longer but nothing came to mind as she made her way to the kitchen.

"Good morning, Señorita Shannon," Maria greeted. "I've fixed some flapjacks for Toby. Would you like a stack?"

"Please," Shannon said with a smile. She propped her cane on the chairback and sat across from Toby who seemed to be in a bit of a hurry this morning. He'd shoveled flapjacks into his mouth until his cheeks bulged. "Are ye afraid somebody is gonna take yer food this morning?"

It took a moment before he could clear his mouth to speak. "Nope. They sure are good this morning," Toby said, but didn't bother to look up.

"Do ye think ye can stop a moment tae say good morning?"

Toby glanced up quickly, barely meeting her eyes. "Mornin'," he managed then looked back to his plate.

Shannon sipped her tea while she studied the child. The warmth felt good in her throat. Toby seemed strange this morning. Not his normal chatty self. Usually Molly was the one-word child. Speaking of Molly .... "Where is yer sister?"

Toby glanced up from under his lashes. "Don't know."

"Ye haven't seen her this mornin'?"

"Nope."

"Look at me, young mon." Shannon waited until she had his full attention. She didn't like what she saw. Toby looked very guilty. "Where is yer sister?"

"Told you. I don't know."

"But ye know something, so ye better tell me."

This time Toby met her eyes. His brows drew together in an agonized expression. There was strain that shouldn't be there. "But I promised."

"Toby?"

"She ran away."

"What?" Shannon stood so fast she had to place a hand on the table to keep her balance.

Tears streamed down Toby's face. "S--she said she was

going to r--run away last night. A—and she wasn't in her room this morning so I guess she did."

Shannon hobbled around the table and gathered Toby in her arms as he sobbed. Glancing at Maria, Shannon asked. "Will ye send somebody to find Wilson?"

"*Sí*. I'll be back in a moment."

"Stop crying," Shannon told Toby as she rubbed his back. "We'll find her. 'Tis not yer fault."

"I—I should have told you." He gasped for air. "B-but she made me promise. And I didn't think she would do it."

"I understand, but the next time ye think somethin' is wrong, ye come and tell me, ye ken?"

Toby stepped back, dashing the tears from his cheeks with the palm of his hands. "Yes ma'am."

The back door opened and Wilson strode into the kitchen, his familiar red handkerchief tied around his neck. "Good morning, Miss Shannon," he said touching the corner of his brown hat with his finger. "You need something?"

"Molly is missing. Can ye take some men and check around the ranch for me?"

"Sure thing." He nodded. "Don't imagine she's gone far."

Shannon stepped away from Toby. Anxiety gripped her chest as a wave of apprehension swept through her. She clutched the back of the chair for support. "I hope yer right."

Hoping Molly was merely hiding, Shannon, Maria and Toby searched the house. They found nothing. Shannon decided to head outside so they could check around the grounds while the men searched further.

They had just stepped off the back porch when Wilson

rode into the yard with a rider-less horse in tow. Shannon felt her stomach tie itself into a knot.

"That's Molly's horse," Toby cried.

Shannon looked up at Wilson. "What did you find?"

"This here's the horse that Molly usually rides, but we didn't see any sign of her. But there's a note." Wilson slipped his hand into his jacket, "It's written in gibberish, which I don't understand," Wilson said. He leaned over and handed a scrap of paper to Shannon.

Shannon slowly unfolded the paper and began to read. It was written in Gaelic. No wonder Wilson couldn't read it.

> If ye want the lassie tae live, ye need tae bring
> yerself and the jewels to me. Ride North.
> I'll find ye. Be warned that ye'd better not
> bring anyone else or the lassie dies.
> Callum

SHANNON FOLDED the note back up and held it tightly in her fist. "I can read it. 'Tis one of my countrymen who has taken Molly."

"What the hell!" Wilson swore, causing his horse to side-step. "Sorry, ma'am."

Shannon felt the blood drain from her cheeks. This was all her fault. She had put Luke's children in danger. It was up to her to save his daughter. She took a deep, controlling breath before addressing Wilson, "If ye'd be sae kind as tae saddle a horse for me, Wilson. I will take Molly's horse with me."

"Yes, ma'am. I'll get some men and ride with you," Wilson said.

"No!" Shannon realized that she'd snapped at the foreman. "I appreciate the offer, but no one can go with me. I dinna want my countryman tae hurt Molly. Leave Molly's horse.

"After that, what I need for ye tae do is tae go and find Luke and tell him what has happened. I'm quite sure I can get Molly away from the mon who has her. However, if we are not back upon yer return . . . tell Luke the note said tae ride north."

"Señorita, this sounds much too dangerous," Maria protested.

"I'll be fine, Maria." Shannon gave her a half-hearted smile. It was the best she could do. "'Tis my fault he's taken Molly. I--I know what he wants and I plan to get Molly back safe." Shannon looked down at Toby. "Ye will need tae keep an eye on him while I'm gone."

"*Sí.*"

"I don't want you to go," Toby said, wrapping his arms around his legs.

"We huv tae get your sister so ye need to be a big boy."

Shannon went to her room and looked in the lining of her carpetbag where she pulled out her mother's jewels. A necklace and five brooches studded with precious stones twinkled up at her. There was also a ruby ring her mother had always worn, but she'd be damned if she was giving that up, so she tucked it back in the bottom of her bag. If Callum killed her, then maybe Luke could use the ring to get extra money for his family.

She shivered at the thought that Molly had been taken. It was all because of her. This had to stop now. Shannon assumed there was only one more of her countrymen here.

Her father couldn't afford to send many men, so maybe she could stop this danger now. She would give Callum the jewels and, hopefully, he would let her and Molly return home. Since Shannon was married, it was pointless to take her back.

Shannon wasn't sure how Luke would take this. He could be so upset with her that he'd throw her out. But it would be a chance she would have to take. She would never place the children in danger.

Wilson helped Shannon mount. Her foot was still very sore, but she'd have gone to get Molly back even if her foot had been broken.

"I'll be leaving shortly," Wilson said. "I need to give the men some orders. Which way are you headed?"

"I'm heading north. Please dinna have anyone follow me. Callum wouldna hesitate to kill the child."

Wilson nodded. "Good luck, missus."

Shannon rode away from the ranch toward town and headed north across open range. There were hills up ahead and a couple of ravines. She wondered if Callum could be hiding in one of those ravines?

It seemed she had been riding for a long time without spotting Callum or anyone else. Wondering if she was heading the right way, she saw out of the corner of her eye a rider heading for her.

Pulling back on the reins, Shannon waited until Callum reached her. He wasn't wearing his kilt. Instead he looked like any other cowboy in Texas only much larger.

"'Tis about time ye showed up," he snarled. "Follow me."

Shannon rode behind Callum. They wound their way past a couple of small hills and down into a ravine that appeared to have been carved into the ground by a river that had long ago dried up.

After they reached a small cave, Callum dismounted. He moved over to Shannon's mount and jerked her from the horse where she collapsed on the ground. "What's the matter, lass, can't ye stand on yer own two feet?"

"My foot is bruised."

"Wull dinna expect any sympathy from me. I've waited too damned long tae take ye back home." He shoved her toward a small opening in the rocks.

When she entered the darkness, Shannon blinked several times to adjust her eyes. Finally, she spotted a small fire and a bundle tied up beside it. She limped toward the bundle. "Molly are ye all right?" Shannon helped the child to sit.

Molly's eyes were large with fright as Shannon untied the handkerchief from around her mouth. "Are ye all right?"

"Of course she is fine, fer now," Callum grunted. "But that could change at any moment."

"I'm going tae untie her. There is no need fer ye tae keep her tied up. I'll give ye want ye want."

Once Molly's hands were free, she jumped into Shannon's arms and sobbed. "I'm so sorry." Molly cried.

"Now, now. Stop yer crying. 'Twill be fine."

"Did ye bring the jewels?" Callum asked. "How ye could leave your clan in such a state is beyond me, lass. Dinna ye no care fer family?"

"My family died when my mother was killed. Ye know as well as I that my da was responsible, and ye want me tae feel sorry fer a drunken no account. I think not. I did what I had tae do tae survive."

"Did ye bring the jewels?"

"I'll not return home, and I told ye I brought the jewels sae ye'll huv the money ye need tae please my da. Shannon slipped her hand in her pocket and pulled out a small bundle. "Here." She tossed the pouch of jewels to Callum.

"Nay, lass." Callum caught the pouch and peered inside before placing it in his pocket. "He wants ye, too."

Molly sat up straight. "You can't take my mother away!"

"Mother?" Callum looked confused.

"I married her father. It wull do ye no good tae take me back."

"Yer da said tae bring ye back. And that's what I intend tae do."

"I won't go."

"Then I'll kill the lass."

Molly hugged Shannon tighter. Shannon wrapped her arms around the child. "If I go with ye without a fight, wull ye let Molly go?"

"Aye. If ye promise not tae give me any problems," Callum said. "I'm going tae pack up the horse. Dinna get any ideas while I'm gone." He backed out of the cave.

After Callum had gone, Molly turned to Shannon. "You can't go with that awful man."

"I must go. I dinna want him tae hurt ye."

"But you're our mother. We just got you," Molly said with tears in her eyes. "I don't want to lose you."

Shannon's heart turned over with joy. Now she knew what it felt like to be a mother. All mothers protected their young. And Molly had called her *mother* for the first time. If Shannon died now . . . she would die happy. She hugged the child to her. "I dinna want tae leave ye, but I must." Molly cried in her arms. "Listen," Shannon said. "I have an idea."

Molly straightened. "An idea?"

"Do ye think ye can find your way back home?"

"Yes. My horse, Blackie will know the way."

"Good." Shannon smiled. "Wilson found yer horse and I

brought it with me. Ye can ride home and tell them what has happened, and how tae find me."

"I can do that." Molly smiled and gave her a firm nod.

"Now ye can't look happy about our plan. As a matter of fact, I dinna trust Callum. I'll distract him, then ye can jump on yer horse and ride as fast as you can, ye ken?" No looking back.

"Nothing can happen to you."

Shannon smiled. "As I once told yer pa, I'm stronger than I look."

Callum came back. "I was going to head out in the morning, but it looks stormy and will be good for covering our tracks. Ye dinna mind gettin' wet? Any Highland lass should be used to wet." He chuckled as he moved in front of Shannon. "Give me yer hands."

"Why do ye huv to tie my hands?"

Callum laughed. "I dinna trust ye." It didn't take him long to tie her hands, then he jerked her to her feet. "Come on, I'll get the *bairn* after ye."

Shannon glanced at Molly and gave her a slight nod. The child nodded back to indicate she understood what she needed to do.

Shannon hobbled beside Callum who tried to drag her when she stumbled. "If ye remember, my foot is bruised and I canna walk fast," Shannon said.

Once they were outside Shannon saw that it was still afternoon, but it appeared much darker because of the storm clouds. The rumble of thunder could be heard, but still at a distance. She knew how fast storms moved out here, and she hoped that somehow the storm would help her get away.

There was a big boulder separating her and Callum's horses from Blackie.

Shannon hobbled over to her mount. When she glimpsed Molly at the mouth of the cave, Shannon said, "I'll need some help getting on my horse, Callum."

"Ye are a hell of a lot of trouble, lass."

"Ye could always leave me."

"I bet ye'd like that," he said bending down. "Put yer foot in my hands."

"That is the problem. 'Tis my left foot and it hurts too bad tae put all my weight on it. Ye'll have tae lift me by the waist sae I can mount."

Callum tried to shove Shannon up on her horse, but she purposely fell back, knocking him off his feet.

"Ye bitch. I'm going tae tie ye across the saddle," he swore as he pushed Shannon off him. "And I'm going tae kill the *bairn* because of yer stunt."

He yanked Shannon to her feet, and she swayed toward him. His back was to the front of the cave so he didn't see Molly atop her horse. Shannon threw her arms around Callum's neck and yelled. "Ride, Molly, ride!"

For just a moment, the child hesitated, but her courage took over and she kneed her mount and rode off.

"What the hell!" Callum yanked Shannon's arms from around his neck but still held her in a vice-like grip. When he saw the child was getting away, he turned his red face toward Shannon and threw a punch, catching Shannon in the jaw.

Shannon felt the pain as she fell backward unable to catch herself. Her head hit a rock and she knew no more.

16

Luke and his brothers began to clear away vines and bushes under the rim of the large gully where they would be camping tonight. The washout was ten feet below the plane of the prairie, giving them good protection from the oncoming gunfire that would be coming their way tomorrow. On the steep ridge, someone had already cut steps into the side of the bluff so the men could easily fire their rifles, and then descend to reload.

The plan was for the right flank of Captain James Fannin's division to occupy the lower part of the bend extending south. Bowie's detachment would be on the left side of Fannin's. This way the two detachments could aid each other.

It was late in the day when they finished and the men headed to their own camps along the floor of the gully. They had tied their horses behind the ravine where the backside of the river, skirted in timber, would offer protection.

Luke and his brothers had chosen the u-bend of the gully to make their small camp. Here it was one hundred yards wide and gave them plenty of room to move around without stepping on someone else.

Luke leaned back against his saddle, a hot cup of coffee held between his fingers. As he relaxed, he thought of home. His first thoughts were of Shannon and the children. He missed seeing them at supper and hearing about their day. Instead of the comfort of home, Luke sat in a dry gully across from his brothers who had just finished their plates of beans. The aroma of coffee was the only reminder of home.

"Good coffee, George," Luke said. "How long has it been since we've all sat around a fire together?"

"Too long," Travis said with a laugh.

George raised his brows in thought. "At least three years, I reckon. This time it took a war to get us all together again. How loco is that?"

"I think it was when Ruth died," Luke said. "Doubt I was much company then."

"Not a good time." George shook his head in agreement. He propped a rolled up blanket under his head. "Glad you've found someone else. Ruth would have wanted you to be happy. Tell me what your new wife is like."

Luke smiled. Automatically, he pictured Shannon in his mind's eye. He was glad that it wasn't Ruth who had come to mind first. "Shannon is like no one I've ever met. She's a small, but feisty Scot."

"You forgot to say she's pretty," Travis added.

"How did you manage that?" George asked. "How do the children like her?"

"Well, I advertised for an old and ugly nanny. I got anything but." Luke chuckled. "I think she handles the children well because they had become a handful as you both know. However, Molly isn't real happy." Luke took a swallow of coffee. "I think she'll come around though." He leaned forward and placed his empty coffee cup on one of the rocks near the fire. "Molly thinks that we are betraying Ruth. I thought so, too, for awhile so I know how the kid feels."

Travis set his coffee cup down too. "You do realize that you're not betraying her? She'd probably be the first to tell you that you and the kids need someone."

"I do now that you've pointed out the fact a half a dozen times." They all laughed together. It felt good, Luke realized. He felt as if a heavy weight had been removed from his shoulders, and he hoped more laughter would be in his future.

"After Ann has the baby and is feeling well enough to travel, we'll come and visit. Better yet, you can bring the family for a visit."

"Yeah, let's all get together," Luke replied. "But for now let's get some shuteye before tomorrow. You two remember to keep your heads down tomorrow. I want all three of us to ride out of here."

DAMPNESS SETTLED around Luke as he slept, but he didn't know the cause until he woke up the next morning. Fog as thick as mush surrounded them.

He smelled coffee coming from somewhere, but he couldn't see any further than his brothers who were still asleep. "Wake up. We have a problem," Luke called to them.

Slowly George shoved himself into a sitting position. "How are we going to see anyone in this dense fog?" he asked, but didn't receive an answer as grapeshot rang out followed by a couple more shots. The grapeshot shook the pecan trees on the edge of the gully, raining a shower of pecans down on everyone's head.

"I need to take these nuts home," George joked. "Ann can make pecan pie."

They scrambled to their positions along the dirt wall.

The sentinel, Henry Karnes, came running from the end where he had been keeping watch. "They're coming, boys. Better get into position – I got two of them, but it's damned hard to see anybody until they're right on top of ya."

Another figure emerged through the fog and came up behind them. He was running in a crouched position along the gully. They saw that it was Deaf once he drew closer.

"What do they have out there?" Travis asked.

Deaf paused a moment. "Appears to be Lieutenant Colonel Mendoza's infantry. They've set up below our position. Don't figure they will do much as they can't see either, but be prepared." He spit out a stream of brown tobacco juice out, and said, "Remember, they will be firing Brown Bess muskets, which have a maximum range of seventy yards. They'll have to get close to hit us."

"Then we have the advantage with our Texan long rifles since they shoot two hundred yards," Travis said.

"Yep," Deaf said with a chuckle. "But they have two cannons and 275 men."

"No problem." Travis laughed. "Should be easy."

They heard Deaf's laughter all the way down the long gully as he ran to warn the other men.

"You never did have any sense," Luke told Travis. "Look, the fog is starting to clear. I hope your aim is as good as it used to be."

Luke, Travis and George climbed up to see what was

happening. Fifty or sixty Mexican infantrymen began crossing the prairie with a cannon in tow.

"That can't be good," George said.

Bowie came from their right and said, "Keep under cover, boys, and reserve your fire. We haven't a man to spare!"

At three hundred yards in front of their position, the Mexican infantry halted and formed a line with the cannon in the middle. As they advanced toward the Texans position, they began to fire. The Mexicans didn't bother to hide behind anything. Instead they marched in a straight line as taught by Europeans. Suddenly, a cannon ripped the air, but the shots seemed to be going over Luke's head, landing on the backside of the ravine. A little too close for comfort, he thought.

Finally, Bowie shouted. "Fire!"

They began a snipe-and-hide tactic where one man would shoot his Texan long rifle, then come down the steps to reload while another man took his spot. Luke and Travis were working well together as a team. It was a blessing, that all the men were deadly accurate; Luke could see they were cutting down the Mexicans and stopping them in their tracks. But more Mexican troops took the places of the fallen men.

Three times the Mexicans attacked. On the third try, the Texans redirected their fire on the cannoneers. Soon they heard the buglers sounding retreat, and the infantry fell back beyond the Texans' rifle range.

"Come on, men," Bowie called as he climbed out of the ravine. "Follow me!"

Luke and Travis followed. For a short while, it seemed like all hell had broken out with bullets flying over their heads. They quickly captured the abandoned cannon as the men fled. They swung the cannon around and began firing on the retreating Mexican soldiers. Grapeshot killed one of the mule drivers causing his caisson to go out of control and into the enemy's ranks.

The battle was over. The Texans had won. Luke and Travis felt pretty good as they made their way back into the ravine to the cheering men. But Luke stopped short when he saw Wilson, his foreman, standing beside George.

"What's wrong?" Luke asked.

"You need to come home," Wilson said. "Miss Shannon sent me to find you because someone has taken Molly."

"What?"

"Molly ran off yesterday morning. We searched and found nothing but her horse with a note on it," Wilson explained quickly.

"What did it say?" Luke asked.

"Don't know. Couldn't read it, but Miss Shannon could. She seemed to know who the note was from. She said she was the only one who could go after Molly," Wilson explained. "That's when she told me to find you at once."

"Let me get my horse," Luke said. He turned to look at his brothers. "I'll see you two later."

"No you won't," Travis said. "I'm coming with you to help find both of them."

"Don't leave me out," George said, "I'll help, too."

They told Bowie what was going on and wished him luck in San Antonio. Once they found their horses, they began the journey home, making sure not to come in contact with Mexicans. They were able to ride at a good clip, Wilson leading the way.

"What's this about?" Travis asked.

"Some of Shannon's countrymen were trying to find her and return her to Scotland, back to her father. Remember the fellow in the alley? He was one of them. We thought that he might be all there was, but I guess not."

"Damn!" Travis swore. "Well, she's married now and can't go gallivanting off to Scotland."

Luke glanced at George who was riding on his left. They were nearing the turn off for George to go home. Luke pulled his mount up and everyone stopped. "I appreciate your offer George, but I think you need to get home to your wife. You need to be there when Ann has the baby."

"Guess you're right," George said. "But if you do need more help be sure to send word."

"We will." Luke reached over and shook his brother's hand. "Let me know when the baby makes an appearance."

"Will do," George said as he broke away from the group and headed home.

It was late by the time they got back to the ranch. Luke thanked Wilson for finding him so quickly and then said goodnight. Luke and Travis bedded down their horses and fed them before going to the house. It had been a long day and they wanted the animals fresh for tomorrow morning.

"It's too late to do any searching tonight," Luke said. "We will head out first thing in the morning."

"Yeah, I agree," Travis said as they walked toward the kitchen. "I see lights in the kitchen. Maybe Maria will have some leftovers from supper."

"Strange," Luke said. "Everyone should be in bed."

They entered through the back door and placed their hats on the pegs before turning to head into the kitchen. Luke stopped dead in his tracks. "Molly?"

She had been resting her head on her arms, but as soon as he spoke her head popped up. She had been crying. Jumping out of her chair, she ran to him and wrapped her arms around his waist and wailed, "I'm sorry. I'm sorry."

Luke reached down and hauled her into his arms where he returned the hug. "I thought you were missing?" He glanced at Maria and she nodded. "It's going to be all right. Now, sit and tell me what happened while we grab a bite to eat. Are you hurt?"

Molly shook her head.

"She got here thirty minutes ago, Señor Luke," Maria said, then she turned around and began to plate some food for them. "She no say what happen."

"Take your time and tell me what happened," Luke urged his daughter.

Molly sniffed a couple of times and then she told them everything that had happened from the time she left the house. "You have to save Miss Shannon, Pa. That man was mean and he will hurt her."

Luke was so angry he couldn't speak.

"We will find Miss Shannon," Travis said to break the silence.

Luke took a deep breath. "Do you think you can tell me where the cave is located, Molly?"

"I think so, but I can show you easier."

"No. I want to know that you are safe and sound," Luke said. "Travis and I can ride faster without me having to worry about you."

"Promise me that you will bring her back home," Molly sniffed.

It registered with Luke that something had happened to make Molly want Shannon in their lives, which made him glad. "I promise. We will leave first thing in the morning."

"Why can't you go now?" Molly asked.

"There's no moon tonight. We can't see where we're going. It's much too easy for one of the horses to step in a hole and break a leg. Shannon and the man will have to camp for the night, too. We won't be losing any time. So don't worry. They probably don't think anyone is following them. I'm sure he didn't think you could find your way home all by yourself." Luke smiled and gave his daughter another hug.

"We will bring her home. I promise."

17

*S*hannon woke up with a blinding headache, trying to remember where she was and what had happened. Rain dripped off the end of her nose. Strange, but she was in an upside down position . . . suddenly, she remembered the events leading up to this moment. Shaking her head to get the hair out of her eyes, she realized she'd been thrown across a saddle. Her chest ached from the pressure of her body being supported by her chest. Damn that Callum! She wanted on her feet again. "Let me up! Let me up!" She screamed as if the hounds of hell were after her. She thrashed her body the best she could so that the horse half reared up.

It was only a couple of moments before she was dragged roughly from the saddle and thrown to the wet ground as the rain fell in sheets. She gasped for air until she caught her breath. Where were they? She glimpsed a river below them, but she had no idea where they were, or if Molly had managed to find her way home to send help.

"I'm getting damned sick of ye, lass," Callum grumbled. "However, I'm glad tae see ye huv joined the living again."

"Ye could always let me go," Shannon suggested.

"Dinna think so." He shoved her up on the horse.

"At least untie my hands."

"I'm not daft, lass. Ye can ride like this, or I can throw ye back over the horse like a sack of potatoes again. "

Shannon frowned when he handed the reins to her.

"Dinna give me any trouble. Let's get going. And dinna think that the lassie wull save ye. Nobody can track us in this rain."

Shannon didn't doubt that statement. Even the ground was becoming soggy as the rain lashed down. Thunder rumbled overhead.

They had ridden no more than thirty minutes when a bolt of lightning hit one of the bald cypress trees near them. The ground shook. Callum's horse stopped short, pitching Callum out of the saddle and down the ravine. Shannon's horse reared tossing her to the right. She hit the ground so hard it knocked the breath out of her. Both horses bolted. Once she'd caught her breath, she called out to them, but they didn't bother to stop.

Shannon crawled to the ravine's edge and peered over the side. Callum's body lay broken with his limbs twisted at wrong angles. She wouldn't have to be worry about him ever again. At the moment, she had a bigger problem. What was she going to do without a horse and her hands tied?

She could lie here and feel sorry for herself, or she could have the gumption that she'd always used to survive. She wanted to climb down the ravine and get her mother's jewels, but she was afraid she'd never make it back up the hill. The jewels would have to wait until she could find help. But how would she remember this place? She reached down and ripped a scrap of material off her skirt and tied it to the limb of a tree so it wouldn't blow away. If she should survive, then she could find the place again.

With supreme effort, Shannon found a sharp stone and rubbed the ropes across the edge until they gave way and freed her hands. Then she got to her feet and started walking to what she hoped was one more step closer to home. She walked and walked. Her clothes were soaked and heavy from the rain. Only determination kept her going.

After a while the rain stopped, making walking a little easier but not much. She limped one step at a time until nightfall came. She knew that she should try to move on, but she could go no farther. She glanced down at her bruised ankle. It had turned a dark bluish color and was swollen, and it hurt like hell when she touched her foot. She would have to stop and this was as good a place as any, she thought looking around.

As the sky grew darker, the air became cool, causing Shannon to shiver in her damp clothing. At least it had stopped raining but that was the only good thing she could say at the moment.

She needed a fire but she didn't know how to make one, besides everything was wet. The only warmth came from her wet coat.

A wolf howled in the distance and drew her attention away from being cold. Without a fire, the animals would sense helpless prey, and she didn't want to be their next meal. However, this was no time to lose her head. She needed to think fast as two wolves howled this time.

Spying a small group of large boulders, she limped to the rocks. Picking up a long stick, she jabbed around the rocks to make sure there were no snakes hiding. It would not provide much protection, but, at least, her back would be protected. If an animal came for her she could fight them off with the stick, she hoped. It wasn't much, but it was all she had. She also gathered some tumbleweed, and placed them in front of the rock opening, and weighed them down with smaller stones so they wouldn't blow away.

Again the eerie sound of wolves make the hair stand up on Shannon's neck. She prayed they were not close. She also prayed that they couldn't sense her fear.

Her face hurt from the sun and windburns. Exhausted and bewildered, Shannon's head felt as if it were twice the size it should be, and she couldn't hold it up anymore. She was freezing cold. Curling one arm under her head to give her a little cushion from the rock, she tried to get comfortable. She gripped the stick with the other hand, hoping she wouldn't have to battle a pack of animals tonight. As a heavy weight settled upon Shannon, she knew she might never make it back to the ranch, but at least she didn't have to worry about any of her countrymen looking for her.

She would miss Luke and the children. Hopefully, they would remember that she loved them. As her eyelids drifted closed, she thought if ever she needed a miracle, it would be right about now.

Where are you, Luke?

❧

LUKE AND TRAVIS traveled most of the day before they reached the cave. Molly had given them specific directions so they hadn't wasted any time looking for the opening, but the cavern was empty.

"Now what?" Travis asked.

"Let's look around and see if we can find some clues to which way they went."

Both men scoured the rocks looking for a sign and praying for a miracle.

"Remember, it was raining." Travis said.

"I know, I know, but there has to be something," Luke said, then his eyes landed on something. "Look." It was a small piece of fabric. "This is from Shannon's skirt. Maybe she left us some clues."

Travis pointed to a rusty-colored stain on the edge of a rock. "That looks like blood."

Luke bent closer and picked up several long, red strands of hair. "She's been hurt. That son of a bitch, I'll kill him!"

"I'm surprised the hair didn't wash away in the rain," Travis said, then looked up. "Guess the overhang protected the rocks."

"We've got to find her," Luke couldn't hide the urgency in his voice as he turned to mount his horse again.

"Look," Travis said, gaining his brothers attention. "I want to find Shannon too, but it's dark and the horses need to rest. I'm going to take them down to the river for water. You build a fire so we can at least have some coffee. They can't travel at night without moonlight, and they don't know the land like we do."

Luke sighed knowing his brother was right. They had ridden hard the day before and then today on the same mounts. "We leave first thing in the morning."

"Agreed." Travis said as he walked the horses down the bank toward the water.

The fire was small but enough to keep critters away from them. Luke had found some beef jerky in his saddlebags. He and Travis shared the jerky with their coffee. Since Luke was sure that they would find Shannon the first day, he hadn't bothered to pack any food.

"Which way do you think they rode out?" Luke asked.

"The way I figure it," Travis said scratching the stubble on his chin, "they're both greenhorns. Of course, Shannon wouldn't have any say, but neither one of them are familiar with Texas. I'd say they would follow the Guadalupe River and then head toward town for the stage."

"You're probably right. Let's hope we find them in the morning."

Luke leaned against his saddle and dozed, but he really didn't get much sleep. All he could think of was Shannon. This was harsh country for a woman. He couldn't bury another wife. He hadn't realized how much she meant to him until he had gone to battle. Now all he could do was think of her, and how he wanted to hold and kiss her. He hadn't even told Shannon he loved her, but that was going to change just as soon as he found her.

THE NEXT MORNING, they followed the river, riding along the upper cliff. They had just dodged a group of scrub oaks when Travis said. "Look up ahead, I see something."

When they got closer they both dismounted and tied their horses to a tree. "Look it's part of Shannon's skirt. She made it this far," Luke said then added, "At least she's alive."

"I'm sure she is out here somewhere. Look at the cliff." Travis pointed. "Looks like it gave way."

Peering over the edge of the cliff, Luke said. "There's a body sprawled next to the river. Appears to be a man from the size of him. Let's go down and get a better look."

They slid down the embankment and landed with a soft thud. Luke brushed off his clothes and walked over to the prone body. "Look at the red hair. Looks like Shannon's hair." Luke reached down and rolled the man over. "He's a big one. Doesn't look like he's from around here. Search his pockets on that side, and I'll do the same."

"What's this?" Travis pulled out a black pouch. Carefully, he unwrapped it. "Damn."

Luke stared at the brooches and jewels worth a small fortune. "Shannon said her father was after jewels. But I figured it was a locket and a ring. This appears to be a small fortune. She didn't have to be a nanny." Now Luke wondered why Shannon had stayed with his family when she could have gone anywhere.

"Lucky for you, she chose to be your nanny," Travis said what Luke had been thinking.

He took the bundle from Travis and slipped it into his coat pocket. "So this must be her countryman, but where is Shannon?"

Travis looked up at the cliff. "Appears that a chunk of dirt broke off. Maybe his horse threw him. That would explain the broken neck. Maybe Shannon got away and we can find her."

"Let's go." Luke turned and started back up the cliff. Once he reached the top, he noticed footprints. "Look at this, Travis. You have more experience in tracking than I do. The footprints are small. It has to be Shannon!"

"Strange," Travis said. "Do you suppose Shannon was thrown, but was lucky enough not to go down the cliff?"

"Well, we know she didn't go over the cliff," Luke said. They mounted once again and followed the tracks.

A couple of hours had passed when they spotted two horses grazing. Travis went to round up the animals, while Luke kept on the tracks. He said a small prayer that Shannon was all right and thanked God there hadn't been any rain to wash away the tracks.

"I can't believe she made it this far, and on a bruised

foot," Luke said with an unpleasant feeling curling in his belly. "It appears she is dragging one foot. I'm praying she is still alive."

"You've got one tough woman," Travis commented. "Most women would have given up a long time ago."

Just then they heard the howls of wolves. "That doesn't sound good," Luke said and spurred his horse into a gallop. They followed the sounds of the wolves until they came to a group of rocks. Luke pulled out his rifle and fired up in the air to scare the animals. Five of them scattered; however, the biggest wolf was determined to get something or someone from within the rocks.

Luke moved to the side with his horse and taking careful aim so as not to shoot into the rocks, he took one shot and the wolf collapsed. Luke heard something. "Listen."

"Help."

"Look." Travis pointed. "Behind the sagebrush."

"I see it." Luke dismounted and ran for the rocks. He yanked back the tumbleweed and found Shannon clutching a big stick. She appeared extremely pale, but alive.

"Ye found me," she said in a weak voice.

"Yes, sweetheart," Luke said. He pulled Shannon out of the small crevice that she had managed to squeeze herself into. "Are you all right?"

"No. My head hurts and my foot is swollen. That wolf thought I was its next meal, and he was trying verra hard tae eat me," she said as Luke pulled her to her feet. Unable to stand, she collapsed against him. All her muscles were stiff. "I dinna think that ye'd find me."

Shannon clutched the front of Luke's shirt and asked, "What aboot Molly?"

"I'll always find you," Luke said with a smile. He hugged

Shannon. "And Molly made it home. She is safe, thanks to you."

He brushed Shannon's hair back and noticed she was very hot with fever and her face was raw from the wind. "Travis, she has a fever. Hold her so I can mount. We need to get her home."

Travis took Shannon in his arms, "You're one brave young woman."

"Nay. I did what I had tae do," she said. "He wull no be bothering us anymore," her words faded as she passed out.

"She's fainted," Travis said as he handed her limp body to Luke.

Luke took Shannon into his arms. "It will make the ride home a little easier on her. She must hurt all over. "Let's ride. You can take the other horses."

THREE DAYS HAD PASSED since they had returned to the ranch. Shannon had a raging fever, and she was unconscious most of the time.

The doctor said she was suffering from exposure and there wasn't much he could do. Her body needed to heal itself. He assured Luke that it wasn't scarlet fever like Ruth had; however, it was serious nonetheless.

Luke faithfully sponged Shannon's body with a damp cloth even though Maria had said she would do it. Shannon was his responsibility, and he wouldn't leave her until she was well. He'd only left Ruth for an hour and she had died. He wouldn't make the same mistake again.

Travis had to leave to report to the rangers, but he promised he'd come back as soon as he could. Luke understood.

Luke lay his head on the side of the bed, trying to get some rest. He was so tired. If only he could get a few minutes of rest then he'd feel a little better.

The door opened and Molly came into the bedroom. She placed a small hand on Luke's shoulder.

He sat up looking about disoriented. "What? Is something wrong?"

"She's going to die just like Ma, isn't she?" Molly said in a choked voice.

Luke slipped his arms around Molly. "Shannon will not die," he said firmly. "She told me, herself, that she's was much stronger than most women."

"But she isn't awake. I haven't heard her talk since you came home."

"It's because of the fever. We need to make the fever go away, which is why I've been placing cool, wet cloths on her forehead."

"Just like Ma."

"No," Luke said quickly. "Your mother had scarlet fever. Shannon just has a fever.

"Do you think a wet cloth will really help?" Molly asked. "When I'm hot, I take a cool bath."

Luke glanced at his daughter. "Molly you are a genius! Why didn't I think of that? Get Maria to fill the bathtub, and we'll give it a try." He hugged his daughter then swatted her backside as she left the room.

A short time later, Luke lowered Shannon into the cool water. She moaned. He took it to be a good sign. He had sent Molly to fix him something to eat while he bathed Shannon, more or less to give Molly something to do and keep her from worrying so much.

He poured cool water over Shannon's head, which caused a lot of sputtering from the patient. He smiled. She was fighting. She wasn't going to give up easily. He wasn't going to lose her. They had an entire life ahead of them.

Her body did feel cooler, he thought as he pulled her out of the water and wrapped her in a towel. After he carried her back to the bedroom, he slipped a thick linen nightshirt over her so she wouldn't have to be under any cover.

"Hot," Shannon murmured.

It was the first word she had spoken in three days. He smiled and thanked heaven for the small sign that he was doing the right thing. There was no way he could lose this woman. She was like a breath of fresh air that had blown into his life when he wasn't looking.

Luke stroked the back of her hand and noticed how soft her skin was. "I love you, Shannon. You need to wake up so the children can tell you what they have been doing." Still no response. Luke felt defeated, but he wouldn't give up. He was going to will her to open her eyes.

Several hours went by as Luke talked to Shannon, telling her about the ranch and about how empty his life would be without her. His uneaten food lay on a plate on the bed stand but he didn't care. His wife was the most important thing.

He heard someone sniff. He turned and saw Toby and Molly standing in the doorway already dressed for bed. Luke waved them into the room. "Are you two going to bed?"

Molly nodded and Toby said, "I want to tell Miss Shannon goodnight."

Luke moved away from the bed. "I think she'd like that."

Toby scrambled up on the bed and placed his small hand on Shannon's face. "Miss Shannon, I want you to wake up. I miss you. I bet I can even beat you at hopscotch, but it isn't much fun without you." He waited for a minute . . . when there wasn't a response, he leaned over and kissed her on the cheek, tears streaming down his cheeks.

Luke reached over and scooped Toby up in his arms, hugging the child to him and wishing he could ease Toby's pain. Luke was feeling the same way inside.

Molly leaned over the bed and placed a kiss on Shannon's cheek. "I have learned my figures like you wanted me to, and I read my book. I love you, Miss Shannon. Please don't leave us." Molly was turning to leave when she heard a groan and turned back. Shannon's eyes were open.

Molly laughed between her tears and grabbed Shannon's hand. "Pa, she's awake!"

$\sim$

SHANNON GAZED at Molly's tear-streaked face. Her eyes felt like sand was in them, but she could still see the child and she didn't want Molly to cry. "I love ye, too, Molly," Shannon whispered then added, "What's 2 plus 2?"

Molly giggled. "4."

Toby wiggled out of his father's arms, then ran back to the bed and scooted up beside Shannon. "Toby," Shannon said is a soft voice. "I love ye, too. Now go tae bed, and I'll see ye in the mornin'. I promise I'll be here when ye awake."

Shannon closed her eyes. The effort to keep them open was too much, but her heart was happy. She felt as though she was coming out of a black hole. How long had she been in bed? She seemed to hurt all over. A cool damp cloth touched her head and helped eased the pain. Slowly she opened her eyes again.

She saw Luke bent over her with tears on his cheeks. "Huv I died?"

"No, sweetheart. You're very much alive. I'm glad to see your eyes open at long last."

"Water," she managed to squeak. Her throat was so dry that it was hard to talk.

Luke held her up so she could sip some water, and then he gently let her back down. She was glad as her head pounded in a sitting position.

"Have I been asleep?"

"Not exactly asleep but you have been unconscious for four days."

"R—Really?" Shannon could tell she was getting tired again. "That's why my head hurts."

"You still have a fever. However, you're not as hot as before so you are getting better, even if you don't feel that way at the moment."

"I told ye that I wouldn't die on ye," Shannon said and tried to smile, but she wasn't sure how well that worked.

Luke smiled. "Yes, you did."

"I heard everyone but ye tell me they missed me."

"That is because you were out cold, sweetheart, when I told you I missed you, along with a lot of other things."

"Such as?"

"That life wouldn't be the same without you."

"Oh," she said in a disappointed soft voice. "In that case, I'll go back tae sleep." She started to close her eyelids.

"And I love you very much," Luke added quickly.

She opened her eyelids once more and smiled at Luke with what she hoped was love in her eyes. "Are ye saying, Luke Griffin, that yer my cowboy?"

"Now and forever," he said, and then he leaned over and kissed her softly on the lips.

"'Tis aboot time. Ye look dead on yer feet. I bet I'd get well a lot faster if ye were in bed holding me."

Luke couldn't get undressed fast enough. "Your request is my command."

Once Luke was snuggled next to her, Shannon's last thought was that, at long last, she'd found the family she'd always wanted.

And at long last, she had her cowboy now and forever.

AUTHOR NOTE

I hope you enjoyed Shannon's story and look forward to the next story in the series. I thought many of you might like to see a chapter of SOUTHERN SEDUCTION, so I have enclosed the second chapter and hope you enjoy. The first chapter was woven into Shannon's story. If you would like to keep in touch here are my links. And as always...thank you. I love to hear from readers -

http://www.bkj1608@juno.com

Follow me - below...

https://www.goodreads.com/goodreadscombrenda_jernigan

https://www.facebook.com/bkjbooks

http://www.brendajbooks.com

https://twitter.com/bkj1608

https://www.bookbub.com/authors/brenda-jernigan

ABOUT THE AUTHOR

Brenda Jernigan is a bestselling author. Her books have been nominated for many awards - Book Seller's Best Award, The Maggie Award, and The Holt Medallion Award. Publishers Weekly said, "Brenda Jernigan writes Romance, Adventure and Magic."

She grew up living the life of a tomboy – climbing trees, playing ball, and excluding starry-eyed romance from her daily repertoire. Brenda discovered the love of books while taking her son to Story Hour at the local library -- she was hooked. She set an ambitious goal and began work on her first novel. She continued to write six more novels in rapid succession. She figured having the same birthday as Ernest Hemingway couldn't hurt.

She is a member of RWA, NINC, PAN, PASIC, and Outreach International Romance Writers where she was President. Her books have been printed in several languages and her last book "Southern Seduction" written under the name of Alexandria Scott was printed in Russian.

If you have read and enjoyed the book, please leave a review on the vendor's webpage. Nothing sells books more than word of mouth. Thank you in advance for reading my books.

Follow me- below...

http://www.brendajbooks.com

https://www.goodreads.com/goodreadscombrenda_jernigan
https://www.bookbub.com/profile/brenda-jernigan
https://www.facebook.com/bkjbooks
https://twitter.com/bkj1608
http://www.amazon.com/-/e/B001KI2LIK

ALSO BY BRENDA JERNIGAN

New Release January 1, 2021

THE DEVIL'S LAIRD

Roderick, Warlord of Kirkurd is driven by revenge and guilt.
When his holding was attacked, his wife ravished and slain, and
his son lost to him, the goodness within Roderick died. Now he
is known as the Devil's Laird. Revenge will be his.

The Ladies Series

THE DUKE'S LADY

LOVE ONLY ONCE

THE WICKED LADY

CHRISTMAS IN CAMELOT

The Misfit Series - Westerns

DANCE ON THE WIND

UNTIL SEPTEMBER

WHISPERS ON THE WIND

SEPTEMBER STORM

THE CHOICE

BLACK MAGIC

DIAMOND IN THE ROUGH

THE MISFITS

STORMY PASSION

SOUTHERN SEDUCTION

WESTERN SEDUCTION

e-mail - bkj1608@juno.com

webpage -www.brendajbooks.com

Follow me on Twitter - @bkj1608

A PEEK AT SOUTHERN SEDUCTION

*H*er journey had finally reached its end.

Brooke Hammond's spirits rose as she and Mr. Jeffries neared New Orleans. Though she'd only caught glimpses of the city as they traveled via the main thorough-fares and straight out of town, she liked what she saw and looked forward to returning to town once she'd settled on the plantation.

Brooke settled back to enjoy the remainder of the ride. It had been a long trip, and she had grown weary of traveling and living out of a trunk, but she tried not to complain. It wouldn't be much longer now.

The country was lovely with the lush trees and fields that Mr. Jeffries had described as sugarcane and cotton.

Brooke pressed her dainty white handkerchief to her forehead. She noticed a vast difference between the air in New Orleans and New York. There was always a hint of moisture in the air here. That, in combination with the extreme heat, made her skin feel clammy.

Finally the carriage began to slow, and through the carriage window Brooke caught her first glimpse of a sign announcing they were about to enter Moss Grove Plantation. Her breath caught in her throat. She couldn't seem to utter a single word as a hundred thoughts rushed into her head all at once.

At last she'd have her very own home, a home that was hers permanently, not for just a little while. Most important, she would be the mistress. She'd never have to depend on anyone else's decisions ever again. A home meant much more to Brooke than money. It was something that she had never had. The years growing up in a boarding school were the closest thing to home she could imagine.

All her dreams were about to come true.

The mansion wasn't yet visible when the carriage swung between the octagonal, brick *pigeonniers* positioned on either side of the drive, so seeing her new home was once again delayed. However, the red dirt driveway was smooth and unrutted, demonstrating that a great deal of care had gone into the preparation of the plantation. She could just imagine what the house must look like.

So far, Brooke had to admit that she liked what she'd seen of America compared to England's damp cool days.

Today the sky was beautiful and clear, though the heat would take some getting used to with her thick British blood. Perhaps with fall approaching, the days would be very pleasant. "The trees here are a bit unusual and very wide, don't you think?" Brooke asked Mr. Jeffries who sat across from her.

He slid back the leather flap on the window. "I believe they are called live oaks. They grow very large and wide," he explained. "And I see a few pecan trees mixed in the group."

Huge live oaks, of which Brooke had already counted twenty, lined the long drive on either side. As the carriage traveled down the lane, the limbs were laced overhead like fingers, dripping with a queer, graybeard-like growth that Brooke had never seen before.

She pointed out the window. "What is the greenish-gray substance?"

Jeffries again peered out the window, and this time smiled. "It is Spanish Moss. Quite common in this part of the country, I believe." He leaned back in his seat. "The moss actually lives on the tree limbs and will spread from tree to tree. It resembles a graybeard and can absorb water ten times its weight. Quite lovely, I think."

"Yes, it is. Perhaps it's where the name of the plantation came from," Brooke murmured. The moss was indeed beautiful, yet it also gave her an eerie feeling. She hoped it wasn't a warning sign that something sinister lurked ahead. A slight chill shuddered through her as she shook the qualms from her mind. Surely the staff would welcome a new mistress.

When she thought she could bear the suspense of waiting no longer, a magnificent plantation house came into view. A two-story, white house with one-story wing pavilions on each side sat gracefully at the end of the sweeping circular carriageway, and it was hers . . . all hers.

Ten white columns stood at attention across the front like soldiers, adding to the feeling of grandeur. There was a full second-floor balcony, making for a lovely veranda supported by the columns and bordered with wrought iron. Two curved staircases in the shapes of half moons led up to the main floor. Brooke could only gape, awestruck at the opulence she saw before her.

"I see you're impressed," Mr. Jeffries commented quietly.

"This is not like anything I've ever seen before," Brooke whispered, afraid that someone would pinch her and wake her up from this wonderful dream. How could she be so lucky? "I'm surprised that Jackson stayed in England when he had such a magnificent home and this beautiful sunny weather."

"I believe he had other ideas for Moss Grove."

The carriage pulled to a stop before the wide steps at the front of the house. The driver swung down, opened the door and let down the step for them.

Brooke gathered her skirts so she didn't trip, then accepted the driver's hand. She had just stepped down from the carriage when a man came galloping up on a magnificent white stallion, clouds of dust swirled around the horse's hooves. For a moment, Brooke recalled her girlhood dream of being swept away by a handsome prince on a white horse. Of course, the silly child's dream had faded as she'd grown, and she hadn't thought about her prince in a long time.

Until now.

The man riding toward her made an awesome picture as he sat tall in the saddle. He reined in his horse a few feet away from them, but said nothing, allowing Brooke another moment to look at him. He was dressed in riding clothes, but he wore no jacket as most gentlemen did, just a white billowing shirt and black riding breeches. His blue eyes flashed, then narrowed as he leaned forward in the saddle and looked down as if they were insects to be trod upon.

The sun played on his sun-streaked hair, wind-tossed and rather long, Brooke noticed as he examined them. In spite of his superior attitude, his bronzed skin gave him a rakish air that Brooke found quite appealing.

She really shouldn't be ogling him, but she couldn't help herself. He was truly breathtaking.

Back in England, the gentlemen she had known had always been pasty and white dandies, most of whom had been old enough to be her father.

But not this one.

He was handsome, recklessly so, and he simply took her breath away. She wondered who he was.

The overseer, perhaps? *Entertainment?*

She could only hope.

"Jeffries," the man muttered curtly, finally acknowledging them. He dismounted and tossed the reins to a young stable boy who had come trotting up while Brooke had been looking at the man. "I had word that you were coming, but I wasn't expecting your wife."

Brooke noted that the stranger had a deep, commanding voice, but she almost laughed out loud at the notion that he thought she was Mr. Jeffries's wife.

"Travis," Jeffries said as he extended his hand. "It has been a long time since I last saw you. You look well."

"As do you," Travis commented, then glanced at Brooke. "Will you introduce me to your lovely companion?"

"Certainly. But she isn't my wife." Mr. Jeffries motioned toward Brooke. "May I introduce you to Brooke Hammond."

Travis lifted her hand to his lips then kissed the back ever so lightly, just enough to make chills sweep over and through Brooke's body. For some odd reason her pulse raced while he murmured, "My pleasure, Miss Hammond." He turned back to Jeffries. "I presume then, that she is your fiancée?"

"Certainly not," Jeffries answered. "She is a friend of your father's."

Travis's gaze was riveted on her, then moving over her body slowly. He stopped abruptly as he glanced back to the solicitor. Travis's brows drew together. "My father? I'm afraid I don't understand."

Brooke had a hard time tearing her eyes from Travis's compelling gaze, but she, too, turned and looked at Mr.

Jeffries. "His father?" Brooke repeated. "Pray tell, who is his father?"

Jeffries' face turned a bit red before he answered, "May I present Travis Montgomery, Jackson's son."

Brooke couldn't hide her startled look as she said, "Jackson never said anything to me about a son." What she didn't add was *...and if he had a son why did he leave the plantation to me?*

"Madam, that does not surprise me one bit," Travis snapped, his eyes turning cold. Evidently, Travis Montgomery wasn't any happier than she was about this turn of events because the interest she'd noted only a moment ago had disappeared as his next words were directed to Mr. Jeffries. "What is she doing here?"

Brooke hated to tell him, but he really wasn't going to like the answer.

THE NEXT HOUR passed slowly as Jeffries tried to calm Brooke and Travis down to where they were not shouting at each other. Neither had taken the news well at all.

It seemed that Brooke's plantation had come with a few conditions attached to it, and one of those conditions was now glaring at her across the library table. She'd been rushed inside so quickly that she hadn't had a chance to observe the interior of the house. They had been ushered straight into the library which acted as Travis's study. It was dark just like the owner.

Since Travis had turned to whisper something to Mr. Jeffries, Brooke took the moment of silence to glance around the room, trying to get a feel for her adversary. The room was well appointed and very spacious. One wall held nothing but books. Evidently, Travis liked to read or at least he wanted to give the impression that he did. A marble fire-place was on another wall, and above the mantel hung a large oil painting of a stern-looking gentleman Brooke didn't recognize.

The only bright spot in the room was the French doors located behind his desk.

Her gaze shifted back to her immediate problem, Travis Montgomery, as Mr. Jeffries tried to explain to Travis that Brooke had inherited half of Moss Grove, and they would be able to work everything out if he'd just listen.

"Over my dead body!" Travis shouted at Jeffries. Travis's eyes were cold, his expression a mask of stone as his gaze settled on her face.

"That can be arranged!" Brooke shot back at the arro-gant cad she was beginning to wish she'd never laid eyes on. Who did he think he was, shouting at her? And why hadn't Jackson ever mentioned that he had a son? To think that she'd found him handsome, reminiscent of her prince -- this man might be a devil, instead. His profile was strong and rigid and she had a strong feeling that he never gave an inch in any argument.

"Get out of my house," Travis said through clenched teeth, his voice strained as if he were barely controlling his temper.

Brooke sensed there was more to Travis's rage than just her sudden appearance, but she wasn't going to cower. Instead, she lifted her chin. "Your house?" she challenged. This man...this... this adversary didn't know her very well -- that was stupid, he didn't know her at all -- but if he thought his shouting was going to get her to leave, he needed to rethink his strategy. Brooke wasn't about to be intimidated by him or any man for that matter.

"Perhaps," she said in her perfect British accent, "you

were not listening. The plantation belongs to both of us, so you had better get used to reality," she informed him, feeling just a little bit pleased that Mr. Montgomery didn't have an immediate retort for her. He didn't appear to be a man who liked to lose at anything.

Well, neither did she.

Instead, he glared at her for a long moment before turning his gaze back to Mr. Jeffries, who sat, looking completely exasperated, at the end of the table, his hands folded over the paperwork in front of him.

"I knew my father hated me . . ." Travis paused, a strange look flashing across his face. "Apparently, I didn't know how much," he said more or less to himself as he lowered his tall, incredibly formed body back into his chair.

The solicitor cleared his throat, before saying, "If you are both finished with your shouting match, I shall continue with the reading of Jackson's will." Jeffries peered over his spectacles at both of them and waited patiently for them to acquiesce.

Finally, they each gave a quick nod.

Travis shoved away from the table. "Before you continue," he said, "I need a drink. Do you care for anything?" His question was directed toward Jeffries.

The solicitor shrugged and nodded, then turned back to his papers.

Travis started for the liquor cabinet located next to the wall when Brooke spoke, "It's quite apparent that your father never taught you any manners either."

Travis stopped. Slowly, he turned around, his gaze leveling on her, anger in his eyes. "My father didn't bother to teach me anything at all," he retorted bitterly. He waited a moment, his brow raised a fraction, almost daring her to comment. "Would you care for something, Miss Hammond?"

Brooke smiled, only because she knew it would irritate him further, then she said politely, "Yes, thank you very much. I would like sherry, please." She saw the fire flash in his blue eyes just before he turned away, and she wondered what it would be like to smother that fire out and, perhaps, tame the beast.

Travis Montgomery wasn't something she'd planned on when she'd embarked on this adventure. Not only his very existence, but the way he made her feel. He fired her blood in more ways than one. However, if he thought he was going to intimidate her, then he had better think again.

The duke had never mentioned he had children, and quite frankly, Brooke couldn't blame Travis for being angry, not only with his father, but at her. She knew what it was like to be shunned by a parent, but that didn't mean Travis's disappointment would make her give up her one great chance at happiness.

She watched him from beneath her lashes as he poured the drinks. His white linen shirt pulled across his back when he reached for the crystal decanter. A tall man ... taller than most, he was rough, arrogant, brash as nearly all Americans were, but so intriguing that he held her attention, which was something Brooke couldn't say about most men.

His sun-streaked hair emphasized the darkness of his bronzed skin, and his strong features seem to draw her to him without his ever opening his mouth. *And it was not a good thing*. She didn't want any part of Travis Montgomery. She was finished with men, especially those trying to control her.

Travis handed her a glass of sherry then took his seat.

This is more what I'd had in mind, Brooke mused as she accepted the glass, *someone to do my fetching.*

Mr. Jeffries drank his Scotch. He looked like he needed it more than anyone. He sighed, then, once again, he gathered up the papers in front of him and began to read. "I, Jackson Montgomery, being of sound mind, do hereby bequeath my New Orleans plantation to Brooke Hammond and to my son, Travis Montgomery, equally in hopes that, together, they can run the plantation successfully. If, after one year they have not married, one of them wishes to leave the plantation, then one may buy the other out.

"It is my hope that the Montgomery name will be carried on by my heirs, therefore, my other estates will be held in a trust for the birth of my first grandson. That's correct, Travis. I can see your frown now. Even though I spent little time with you, I did give you my last name, and when you were grown, I provided a place for you and your mother to live. I will have you do two things: first you are to throw a party within two weeks of the reading of my will to announce Brooke Hammond to her neighbors. I wish I could give you my title, but since I was not married to your mother that is impossible. However knowing you, I'm sure you could care less about a title.

"Secondly, I want you to do the proper thing by marrying and having children so that the name Montgomery will continue forward. Brooke will make you a perfect wife and bring the estates to you just that much faster along with money. Be nice to her." Jefferies finished, took a deep breath, then added, "There is one exception."

Brooke's head jerked around. "What?" she snapped at Mr. Jeffries. "I have no desire to marry this man or any other man. It's simply out of the question."

"I don't recall asking you to marry me," Travis snapped,

his words uncoiling like a whip. "It sounds more like you had my father hoodwinked," Travis said. He jerked his gaze away from her back to the solicitor. "What was the exception that you mentioned?"

Jackson took a drink. He looked pale. "If my son chooses to marry someone else and has a son, or his wife is expecting before or by the end of the working arrangement, then he doesn't have to buy Brooke out. The plantation will be his alone and a small sum will be provided for Brooke to travel where she chooses to live. If there is no baby then the original buyout stands."

"Of all the sneaky underhanded deals"-- Travis shoved away from the table.-- "he knew damn well the Moss Grove cannot survive without income from his other estates. Now he wants to dictate my life to the point of when I have to produce an heir. I'm surprised that he didn't live long enough that he could actually be in the bedroom to witness the consummation."

"It is my opinion that Jackson hoped you'd both see things differently," Mr. Jeffries said before Brooke could respond. "Perhaps, with a little time . . ." He paused when he received a withering glare from Travis, but he proceeded anyway. "After all, the two of you have only just met."

"This isn't at all what I had in mind," Brooke said awkwardly. "I've traveled a long way to find that I might not have a home." She cleared her throat. "I doubt that time will help anything."

"Exactly what did you have in mind, Miss Hammond?" Travis inquired, his brow raised. He didn't wait for her to answer. "I'm so sorry for the inconvenience, your highness," he continued. "How do you think I feel? It's been my sweat that has gone into pulling this plantation out of ruins."

Travis stood, his hands braced on the polished, cherry

wood table. He glared at her. "But I will tell you one thing, Miss Hammond. I do not intend to have you interfering with the operation of this plantation. Since my father has so conveniently tied up his money, there is nothing to fall back on. If *we* don't make this harvest of sugarcane a success, then I--we will lose Moss Grove, and you'll be part owner of nothing. Do I make myself clear?"

It was as if he'd thrown ice water in her face, snapping her out of her stupor. Brooke shoved her chair back so quickly it teetered on two legs. She shot him a cold look. "Perfectly!" she spat. "Now, let me tell you something. You might not like this any more than I do, but I intend to make the best of this untenable situation by making this harvest a success."

He sneered. "And what do you know about sugarcane?"

"Not much," Brooke admitted when she really wanted to say, *That it's a hell of a lot sweeter than you!* "But I can learn."

"Then you had better learn fast, Miss Hammond, because harvest time is upon us."

"It's Mrs. Hammond," Brooke informed him, the lie rolling easily off her tongue with ease.

He lifted a brow in surprise. "And where is Mr. Hammond? Or do I still have more surprises to come?"

"Dead, I'm afraid," Brooke answered quickly, her eyes cutting to Mr. Jeffries to see if he'd dispute what he knew wasn't true. Back on the ship, Brooke had decided the minute she sailed from the English shores that she'd pose as a widow, so she wouldn't have to explain why she was no longer a virgin, if and when the time came.

Brooke noticed that Travis didn't bother to express his condolences, but she was quickly learning that the exasperating man was nothing like the Englishmen she'd known. It appeared as if he wasn't going to say anything at all. Apparently, he was waiting for her to speak first. Fine. She'd make an attempt at being pleasant.

"Since we are partners, Travis, why don't you call me by my given name, Brooke." He was beginning to make "Miss Hammond" sound like a swear word.

"That would mean we were friends, Mrs. Hammond," Travis said, then dismissed her completely by turning his attention to Mr. Jeffries. "My father didn't know, but I'm engaged to be married. My fiancée and my mother have traveled north to buy Hesione's trousseau."

"So that's where all the plantation money went," Brooke concluded accusingly.

Travis glared at her as if he couldn't believe that she'd dared to interrupt him. Was his fiancée a meek little mouse who jumped at the chance to please him? "Not that it's any of your concern, but Hesione comes from a very wealthy Creole family and is therefore very wealthy on her own part. However, what money I have isn't enough to pull the plantation through another bad year."

He swung back to Jeffries. "As I was saying, we can be married upon her return, and I'm sure an heir will be forthcoming."

Over my dead body! Brooke wanted to shout, but she held her tongue instead. She had been startled by Travis's marriage announcement. She was hoping for some kind of working relationship with the ill-tempered man. It seemed that there were obstacles to surmount everywhere she turned.

However, this fiancée made matters even more urgent. As soon as what's-her-name returned, Brooke had no doubt that Travis would move quickly to marry the woman. She wondered if he really loved this person, or just her money.

Brooke couldn't imagine him in love with anyone. He seemed too cold, almost dead on the inside.

Of course, Brooke had sworn to herself that she would never marry, but if marriage meant keeping the home she'd just been given, then she would have to reconsider the situation because she had nowhere to go. And she certainly didn't wish to take up the profession she'd left so far behind her. This plantation was her hope, her salvation, and her future.

Brooke wasn't sure how she was going to accomplish the task, but somehow she had to seduce Travis into marrying her before his intended returned. Of course, she had skills and knowledge in the ways to seduce men, but if Travis was truly committed to Hesione, she would have a difficult task of it.

Perhaps, as so many men did, he could be persuaded to stray if he were away from home. With the harvest approaching, she figured she'd never get him to leave the plantation.

Still, she had to think of something.

It would have to be a marriage of convenience . . . her convenience.

She watched as Travis shook Mr. Jeffries's hand. So many possibilities ran through her mind, frustration among them. She had thought all her struggles were behind her, but it seemed that nothing had changed. Her future still depended on the will of a man.

Brooke had promised herself that the moment she'd left the ship everything in the past would stay there and she'd start anew. She had been determined to make her life happy and satisfying. Now, there was one thing standing in her way.

Travis Montgomery.

Brooke sighed. The seduction of Travis Montgomery could prove a real challenge. Her subject didn't look as if he would cooperate in the least. Where men usually were fumbling all over her, telling her how beautiful she was -- words she'd learned to ignore -- Travis had barely given her a second glance. His scowl when he did bother to look at her was hot enough to burn. Now all she had to do was turn those fires of anger into embers of desire.

A slow smile touched Brooke's lips. Since when wasn't she up for a good challenge? Her entire life had been a challenge. Any sensible woman with common sense would pick up her skirts and run away.

The problem was, Brooke wasn't sensible.

When she was through with Travis Montgomery, he wouldn't know what hit him.

Travis headed for the door, but Brooke wasn't finished with him. "Are you going to show us to our rooms, or do I get to chose whichever room I prefer? The master suite, perhaps?" She knew she was being catty, but for some odd reason Travis brought out her need to provoke him. Perchance, she just wanted to see some unguarded emotion in him other than the frosty facade he had, thus far, presented.

Travis didn't answer her. Instead, he jerked the door open and shouted, "Mammy!"

That's how he called his mother? Brooke wondered. How rude. No, wait. Hadn't he just said his mother was elsewhere?

Just a moment passed, and a heavyset black woman appeared at the door. "*Oui*, Mr. Travis. What you bellowin' about so early in the day?"

All right, so Mammy was the housekeeper, but with the

odd name, Brooke wondered if this was the woman who had helped to rear Travis?

Poor woman.

"Please show our guests to their rooms." Travis paused, then added, "And Mrs. Hammond will be staying permanently. Make certain that her room is at the opposite end of the hall from mine."

Well, the line had been drawn, Brooke thought with strange satisfaction.

Travis was making it utterly clear that he wanted no part of her. He didn't bother to glance her way one final time, and his expression was just as distant as it had been all day.

Brooke arched a delicate brow to acknowledge him, but remained silent. She knew too well that words could be used against her. It was best to remain silent and make him wonder. She well knew that Travis would do everything in his power to drive her off the plantation, but Brooke Hammond had no intention of leaving.

She tilted her chin stubbornly upward and smiled to herself as she watched him leave.

Well, Travis Montgomery . . . I'd like to see you try.